Dedication

This book is dedicated to everyone who has helped me throughout the years and to you the reader.

Acknowledgments
Cover design by Elena Grimes
Contributions to editing by Angela Haden

Solstice Criterium Era's
series one volume one
part one

The Creation Council Era

written by
Oyak Muisso Meakezy

CONTENTS

Name pronunciation

Oyak:oo-yah-k
Vollenth:vah-len-th
Helk:hell-k
Baranouke:bara-nuke
Talanock:tala-knock
Nana:nah-nah
Zeon:Z-ahn
Palvore:pal-vore
Palex:pa-lex
Jurew:jure-rue
Jurrisk:jur-risk
Vezoth:v-zoth
Velzeak:vel-zeak
Zeaxis:z-axis
Alakouse:ah-la-koose
Felzer:fell-zear
Velvexs:vel-vex-us
Velkereath:vel-ker-reth
Telver:tell-vear
Talakouse:tala-kouse
Halakouse:ha-la-kouse
Talakaver:tal-ka-vear

Time Conversion
9 days in 1 week
26 hours in 1 day
45 days in 1 month
13 months in 1 year
65 minutes in 1 hour
15 hours into 26 is sunset
65 seconds in 1 minute
585 days in 1 year

Chapter 1 The Start

It all began with a single cell, and it all ends with a life cycle that lasts so many lifetimes. This story begins with the creation of five trillion and thirteen very special beings. These beings were created and then abandoned. After some time, thirteen of them woke up. Following a few failed attempts at waking the rest of the beings up, they decided to create a home for everyone. The beings pooled their inner strengths and desires together, fusing forces and making their desires reality, giving them powers that the other beings could normally never obtain. They called these powers energy, they used their energy to create a circular platform beneath the other beings.

The thirteen molded and shaped the platform into what they desired, a home for everyone. The final product of the being's efforts was a giant circular platform that the beings separated by running a four way crossroad through the surface of the platform. In each corner they created a lush green field where they could look out at the empty space around them. Lining the crossroads, they created a spacious home for everyone, and at the center of the crossroads, they created a tower that stretched above every other building.

Once everything was created, the other beings started to wake up. The thirteen helped the others settle into their new homes and shared some of their energy with them. After a few days, the thirteen who created everything were named leaders, and since then they have been called the thirteen Councilors. The beings accepted their title and settled down in the tower at the center where they made various rules and regulations.

Chapter 2 Contestant

My name is Oyak, and I was one of the first beings to wake up after the city was created. After I was guided to my home, I rested for a few days and then started to explore the city. The city was vast, but after a while I became bored after I had explored all of it. Eventually everyone started to explore their own interests through different hobbies. My hobby was to read, write, and shape metal with and without the aid of heat. The Councilors released a small collection of scrolls, books, and journals after a while and updated it over the years, but I was able to read everything they had shared in about a month. I also read anything that the other citizens were willing to share.

The Councilors, after accepting their roles, rarely walked the city as they did the first few days, but I occasionally saw them sitting out on their balconies, reading, writing, or just looking out over the city. The Councilors were laid back generally, until a citizen broke a rule, and then they were merciless. At the end of each week the Councilors appeared in the courtyard around the tower, and announced any new rules that affected us. They kept to this for a few hundred years, until one day all of them disappeared. The Councilors wouldn't appear again until about thirty years later, when they appeared they announced the retirement policy.

The retirement policy said that every hundred and fifty years one councilor would retire, then the council would announce thirteen citizen's names, who would then train and learn the council's secrets. The citizens would train for twenty six years and then be tested on everything they had learned.

The best citizen of the thirteen would replace the retired councillor, and the ones who lost would have their minds erased to protect the council's secrets.

When the policy was first announced, most citizens started dreaming of becoming a councilor. I wasn't one of them. I always respected the Councilors, but I never wanted to become one before or after the policy. That decision isolated me from the rest of the city and caused me to stop interacting with the other citizens.

My decision against becoming a councilor would change on the morning of the forty fifth selection. Each selection began the same way, early in the morning, when the light was just starting to appear over the city. The First councilor's voice interrupted what we were doing and asked us to come to the towers courtyard. Everyone left their homes and made their way to the courtyard. There we waited for the Councilors to announce the contestant's names.

This selection was different. Usually it took only a few minutes for the Councilors to appear, but this time it took them nearly half an hour to appear. The First councilor was the first to show up. He appeared on the edge of the tower's roof, and the rest joined him after a few minutes. The Councilors used energy to project their voices down to us.

"Welcome citizens to the forty fifth contestant selection. If your name is called then report to the tower's lobby once everyone is dismissed." the First councilor said.

Each councilor said a different name. Out of the thirteen I recognized only five of them, Telver, Baranouke, Talanock, Helk, and me. When I heard my name, I froze and began rethinking my decision against becoming a councilor.

The Councilors continued with other minor announcements, but that went by quicker than I expected, and I was still thinking when the crowd around me started to leave. I hesitated for a moment before starting towards the tower, still deciding what to do.

My thoughts were interrupted by the sight of another of the contestants, Telver. Telver was a citizen that lived a few houses away from me. He was arrogant and put everyone else down around him. Telver was about five feet tall with black hair that was cut short. He was also very pale since he spent most of his time indoors, isolated away from everyone else.

"What do you want Telver?" I asked.

"Once we're inside and the councilor asks for the people to give up, you need to ask to give up." he said.

"Why would I give up when I have a good chance of winning?"

"You have no chance of winning Oyak. Just give up!" he yelled.

"You wouldn't be asking me to give in unless you think I'm a threat. I'll win this Telver."

"You'll regret that decision Oyak. If you give up, I promise you when I become councilor I'll give you anything that you desire."

I pushed past Telver and walked into the tower's lobby. The tower's lobby was a spacious room that showed the true scale of the tower. The room itself was massive with a high curved ceiling that stretched up into darkness. The room was sparsely decorated with only a few tapestries and a few dusty bookshelves that only contained a few tomes.

"Contestant." a councilor said.

"Yes, councilor?" I asked.

"Join the other contestants in line. If you win the selection only then will you have time to explore the tower."

"Yes councilor." I said quietly.

I walked over to the other contestants and took my place at the end of the line. Telver walked in after a few minutes. I expected the same lecture from the Councilors, but they remained silent as he walked over to the front of the line.

"Contestants, please remain where you are and remain silent. The First councilor will arrive shortly." The seventh councilor in line said.

All of us waited in silence for a few minutes, then the wall behind the Councilors shifted and a doorway appeared. The First councilor walked through. The wall returned to normal by the time he had taken his place in line.

"Good. All of you are here. Now before you begin your long journey, I will give all of you a chance to give up before it begins."

After a few minutes of silence, he said "Very well. For the next twenty six years you will be learning all of our secrets. This is not an easy task and some of you will fail. Only one will take the title of councilor once this is done.

The first thirteen years will be completed primarily in the classroom where you will learn the history of the city and the council. The second thirteen will be physical training and energy manipulation, along with all the energy techniques that have been created since the Originals created energy. Follow the Thirteenth to the classroom where you will begin your journey...oh yes...good luck."

Chapter 3 The Vision

The thirteenth councilor in line stepped forward and said, "Follow me, contestants."

We followed him as he led us through the twisting halls of the tower. We walked for about an hour before we finally stopped in front of a pair of white doors. The councilor faced the doors and placed his right palm on one of the doors, and after a second, the doors slid into the wall.

"Enter." he said motioning inside.

We walked inside, and the first thing I noticed was the thick layer of dust on everything. The classroom was void of decoration. At the front of the room were thirteen circular desks, which were made with various materials. Each had very unique and different designs. In the middle of the room were thirteen rectangular tables arranged in a half circle. Each table had three chairs behind it. The back of the classroom consisted of a wall of bookshelves filled with dusty books, journals, and scrolls.

"Sit. There's enough room for each of you to have your own table."

Each of us sat down at our own table, and the councilor began pacing at the front of the room. He slowed in front of the first desk and then walked back over to the last desk and sat on its edge.

"Let's start with something simple. Each of you list as many of the Originals' name and rank as you remember or any combination of both."

Over the next hour all of us listed all the Originals' name and ranks until all of us could list all of them by name and rank.

"Good...very good. It usually takes the contestants the entire day. Good effort although all of you are wrong with over half of them but still good effort."

"What do you mean we're wrong? Every councilor that I listed was an Original." Telver asked.

"The list you **and** the other contestants made contained only three members of the Original thirteen. This is due to the erasing technique we use on everyone multiple times a week if necessary."

"Erasing technique?" I asked.

"Yes. The erasing technique is used when a councilor makes a mistake that affects even one citizen. The council erases that event from all citizens' minds and gives you false memories."

"Why?" I asked.

"Hmm...to ensure long lasting peace is the simplest way to put it. If all the mistakes and difficult decisions made by the council were remembered, then we wouldn't be as popular as we are today."

"That won't last forever." Telver said quietly.

"It's lasted since the eighth selection, so I think it'll last for quite some time." the councilor said.

"So do we have to relearn everything that you erased?" Telver asked.

"Yes and no. The erasing technique doesn't actually erase the memories, it just layers over them with false ones until the old memory cannot be accessed. Now, because of the ancient laws, I can't restore all of your original memories, but I can restore the memories you need for your training."

"How?" I asked.

"I place my dominant hand on your forehead and flow energy into your mind and unlock the parts that you need. Afterwards, we wait a few hours for your mind to adjust to the new memories, which usually means a brief nap for all of you."

"I'll start with you." he said.

He teleported in front of me and placed his right hand on my forehead. I felt a cold tingle run through my entire body and then an intense burst of pain emanated from the center of my head. The pain grew more and more unbearable by the second until I could no longer think. Then everything went blank.

Chapter 4 The Beginning

"Contestants, that's enough rest, time to wake up!" the councilor yelled.

The councilor's voice seemed distant. I opened my eyes but all I saw around me was darkness. The darkness seemed to be moving all around me. I saw a single light appear in the distance, and after a while, I saw twelve more ignite around the first one. The lights transformed into the thirteen Originals and glowed brightly in their chests. More lights appeared all around us, but these lights were faint and barely noticeable. The lights around the Originals faded until I couldn't see any other lights but the Original's. The Originals' lights brightened until they were blinding.

I looked below me and saw the city begin to form from nothing. A thin layer began it all, more and more layers placed on top of the initial layer. After hundreds of layers had been stacked, every layer afterwards had grooves carved into it with places that connected all the layers together. The layering continued until the final layer was placed on top of the connected layers. This layer served as the floor of the city. The crossroad appeared in many different forms until finally it split the top layer into what it is today. The four corners that resulted from the crossroad were left bare while the houses were being made. The houses, like the crossroad, appeared in many different forms. Initially, they were all a different size, but soon all of them became the same and only the arrangement needed to be decided on. The crossroads were expanded to make room for the homes and they were arranged in the way they are today.

The corners were then transformed into the lush green fields that they are today. The tower came last and only after a long while. It started off as a small tower but soon rose until it was taller than every other home they had made. After everything was complete, a thin barrier formed around the entire city, and then the faint lights appeared and began to move.

Everything shifted, and I found myself in a dark room. I saw a man in a pure white cloak talking to a black cloaked being. The man in the white cloak had glowing white eyes, the other one had glowing gray eyes. I saw that the gray eyed being had thirteen beings behind him, a dagger was held by a thin thread of energy to each of their throats. I saw the cloaked beings talking, but I couldn't hear them. Suddenly I felt a sharp pain in my head, and then I woke up in the classroom.

"Good. You're finally awake...it took you a little while longer to process all of the memories than the others."

The councilor walked back to his desk and sat on its edge.

"Alright, now that everyone is awake we can begin. Name all thirteen Originals by name along with their respective ranks."

All of us named the Originals and their ranks all within a few minutes.

"Impressive...I think it's time we truly begin."

Chapter 5 The Beasts

The councilor got up and walked over to the first desk and stared at it for a while.

"Let's start with the life of Alakouse. Alakouse is best known for his unique understanding of how energy works. Alakouse could perform any technique ever imagined or invented. He was known as the main leader of the council, and he took pride in that role. Alakouse was...different than the other Councilors. He seemed to have an advanced understanding of every subject you could ever imagine. When the retirement plan was announced, it was decided that he would be the last to retire. Alakouse wrote thousands of books and scrolls...most of them are kept in the council's private library, and only a handful were released to citizens. The books that were released were rewritten under a different name as one of his last requests before he retired. Any questions so far?"

"Why didn't Alakouse take credit for the books that were released?" Telver asked.

"Well, I suppose that he didn't want the credit...but I honestly don't know. The books he didn't take credit for were also rewritten in a different style in order to mask his unique writing style. Overall, Alakouse was the most involved in all the Councilors' activities as well as the citizens' lives. His dedication to the council has never been repeated by any other councilor since his retirement. Alright, now I want all of you to repeat back to me everything that you've learned today."

After five of us had repeated the lessons we learned over the day, the councilor stopped us and gave us an hour break to process everything.

"Well, we'll continue this tomorrow. The light is just about to fade from the city, and I don't like working through the night on the first day, so let's go."

"How do you know the light is fading, there are no windows?" Telver asked.

"A councilor spends most of their time in the tower, so they usually develop an understanding for time even without a window." The thirteenth said.

The councilor walked over to the door and placed his hand on its surface. The doors slid open and he motioned us to follow as he walked out. We followed him through a few hallways until we reached a dead end.

"Hmm...a councilor who can't navigate the tower he lives in." Telver said in a mocking tone.

"Watch your tone, contestant...I know exactly where I am going. Let's see if any of you are gifted with the partial flow of energy...Smart Mouth, walk to the left corner and place your dominant hand on the wall and wait."

Telver walked over to the corner and placed his right hand on the wall and waited.

After a few minutes the councilor said, "Not so smart now are we?"

The councilor waved his hand and a door appeared and slid into the wall.

"Go rest. You'll need your strength for tomorrow."

Telver entered and the door closed behind him and then transformed back into a normal wall.

"The two quietest amongst you, the the shorter and quieter one in the corner opposite of the smart mouth, the taller and slightly more talkative one in one of the center rooms...now!" the councilor yelled.

I walked over to the center of the wall and placed my left palm on the wall and waited. After a second a door appeared and slid into the wall. I looked over at Helk and saw that he had succeeded as well.

"Impressive...go rest now."

The door closed behind me once I was inside. The room had a simple bed with a single sheet and pillow. In the corner opposite of the bed was a small bookshelf with a candle on top and ten different scrolls inside of metal holding tubes. I walked over to the shelf and picked up the first scroll. Engraved on the side of the tube was the name "Alakouse." I looked again and saw that each of the scrolls had the same engraving. I walked over to my bed, sat down, and began reading.

The first nine were about different creatures that the council and citizens had dreamt of, the last was about a type of meditation that Alakouse had created. In the scroll Alakouse said that he sometimes had to replace his sleep with that type of meditation because of the amount of work he had to complete.

Once I had reread everything a few dozen times, I put each scroll back into its proper tube, and then I laid down and started to review that I had learned today. After a few minutes, I stopped thinking and let my thoughts wander. I eventually started to get tired, so I relaxed and fell asleep.

Chapter 6 Training

The vast majority my time as a contestant followed the same pattern of learning, repeating what we learned back to the councilor, opening the door, reading the scrolls, sleeping, and then starting again. This schedule made my time as a contestant blend together.

The Thirteenth continued teaching us about the Originals lives and their responsibilities, which took about eleven months to finish. We then reviewed everything for the remaining two months. The second year was spent entirely on the secrets of the city. A few times during the second year we were taken out into the city and shown the hidden entrances to the network of tunnels that ran underneath the city. The tunnels ran underneath the surface of the city and connected the tower to each citizen's home along with some hidden rooms underneath the tower. The citizens were usually restricted to their homes while we were out to protect the councils' secrets, but sometimes they were allowed to wander as long as they didn't wander too close to the hidden entrances. When they were allowed to wander they always were whispering something hateful towards us contestants. It was probably jealousy, but it sometimes sounded like true hate. The last day of the second year we were given an extensive exam on everything we had learned throughout the two years. The exam was split up into two sections that included a written section and a verbal section. The written part had questions about the city's construction and the Originals lives, and the verbal part was done one at a time outside in the hall and mainly focused on the locations of the hidden entrances throughout the city, along with how to access them.

The testing lasted for most of the day and once all of us were done, the Thirteenth made an announcement.

"Contestants, over these two years I have taught you the lives of the Originals and the secrets of the city. Today was the last day of my time teaching you, and as of right now, there are eight of you that have scores high enough to become a councilor, but this is only the beginning of your journey and only one of you will become councilor. Good luck, the Twelfth councilor will arrive soon." the Thirteenth said.

The Twelfth, Eleventh, Tenth, Ninth, and Eighth covered the same subject, the twenty six trillion ancient laws. The ancient laws were a collection of all the rules and regulations that the citizens and Councilors had to obey. Anyone who broke the rules were killed. At the end of each day, all of us had to repeat back the general idea of the laws that we had learned that day. The days crawled by slowly and by the end of the eighth year, it felt as though it had been a hundred years. The final eight weeks of the eighth year was set aside for the exam, four for each section.

The Seventh councilor was unique and taught us through examples instead of just lecturing. The Seventh had a vibrant personality and was a good relief from the previous eight years. The Seventh also was the middle councilor so he represented a shift in location where we learned. During his first year, we learned the basic principles of energy control and manipulation, and he performed various energy techniques to show us how energy flows through the body and how various techniques use energy. The second year was when we changed locations. Once the first day of the second year arrived, the Seventh arrived to open the doors, and instead of going to the classroom, we were led to the bottom left field to start learning energy techniques. The Seventh didn't teach us any energy techniques, but he showed us how to manipulate our energy in the way that we would when we were taught them. The citizens were allowed to roam the city, but they weren't allowed on the field, only around it. Every day when we went to the field, we always pushed through a crowd of citizens that were gathered around the edge of the field. The citizens there seemed not to be afraid of or hate us, but respected and revered us. The training on the field made the time pass quickly, and in the middle of the last week of the Seventh's second year, we were guided to the classroom to take the exam. The Seventh's exam was slightly different from the others since it included a third section, the performance section. In the performance section, we had to perform various tasks to show our mastery of energy manipulation.

The Sixth councilor held both his years in the field and spent the first year teaching us more advanced energy control and manipulation. The Sixth's second year was spent introducing the basic elemental energy techniques. His exam was like the seventh's, including the third section.

Fifth, Fourth, Third all taught in the field and taught us various techniques that were useful for the life of a councilor, along with a few more points in energy control. The exam was held at the end of the sixth year and included the third section.

The Second taught us in the field, and for his first year showed us various weapons that Councilors and citizens had made over the years. He also showed us how to use them. For his second year, he taught us how to make the weapons with pure energy. The Second's exam was different than the rest since his consisted only of a performance section.

17

The First taught us nothing. He only told us to train and spar unless he told us something else. The first year all of us spared in small groups, and for most of the second year we continued sparing. But instead of small groups, we sparred as a whole. The last week of the second year the First told us to stop sparring and to create our own techniques to use in his exam. Over that week I created twelve techniques, ten of which I showed off in the field and two that I practiced only within my room in the tower.

At the end of the week, the First announced what his exam would consist of.

"Well...the thirteen of you have grown over these years. In my opinion, there are five of you that have had consistently high exam scores and have showed great promise throughout the entire selection. Although, there are ones like the five in this selection that sometimes never end up as a councilor, so the exams are only used to test you throughout the year and are not the final tests that will determine which of you become a councilor. Later today is my exam, and it is different from the rest since it will be a test of everything that you have learned while on the field. My exam will be a spar between all of you. The spar has only two rules, which are no killing and no breaking the ancient laws. We will return to the tower now, and in a few hours all contestants and Councilors will return here, where your exam will take place."

Chapter 7 The Final Spar

All of us returned to our rooms in the tower and waited for the final spar to begin. Waiting for me in my room were ten new scrolls and a body sized mirror. I looked at my reflection and almost didn't recognize myself. I wasn't as pale as I once was, and I seemed more muscular. I walked past the mirror and grabbed a scroll and began reading. I finished all of the scrolls in about twenty minutes. They were all about a different councilor who had made a significant contribution to the council or the city.

After I had reread them about a dozen times each, I started to meditate. When I meditated, I let my mind wander, but once I found an interesting topic or memory, I stopped and analyzed it until I could describe even the smallest detail. I was interrupted about thirty minutes into it.

"Contestants, report to the field...now." the First Councilor said.

I got up and started walking to the field, taking my time as I walked through the city.

When I finally arrived, I saw that I was only the third contestant to arrive. I joined the others in line and waited for the other contestants. The other contestants took a few more minutes to arrive.

Once the others were in line the First councilor said, "Ahh good. Everyone has arrived...let's begin. This battle will be a final test of sorts...in this battle there is only one rule...no killing...everything else is allowed."

The Thirteen Councilors jumped off of the field and all yelled, "Begin!"

The field was enveloped in an energy barrier. All of us jumped away from each other. I landed by the edge of the barrier and took a fighting stance. All of us were still for a few minutes, just observing each other's strengths and weaknesses. Telver made the first move by charging Helk with a hand and a half energy blade. Helk dodged the initial attack and retaliated with a jab from a dagger. Baranouke and Talanock both ran at me with battle axes drawn. I waited until the last possible second and then I rolled out of the way. Their axes collided and sent each other flying across the field. Once they got up and retrieved their axes, they started again.

I mostly kept to hand to hand combat, using energy only when I couldn't avoid it. The battle continued for a few hours. Over those hours I had only used a small amount of energy. Near the end of the fight most of the contestants were starting to lose focus. Once everyone was at that point, I fully released my energy, performing one of the techniques that I had been practicing in my room for the last week. It was a simple technique. When used on an object, it allowed me to control its motion and move it around. When used on a person, it allowed me to temporarily paralyze them and control their movements. I used it on the other twelve, first paralyzing them, then lifting them up a few dozen feet and slamming them onto the field, knocking all of them out. The technique drained all of my energy and weakened me. I collapsed and passed out from the strain of the technique.

Chapter 8 The Tester

I woke up laying on my back where I had fallen. I got up and noticed that I was the only contestant on the field. About ten feet from me was a lone councilor sitting on the field, staring out into the void. The councilor was wearing a deep brown cloak and was sitting down with his legs stretched out in front of him, the hood of the cloak covering his face. He turned and looked over at me, and I recognized him as the Seventh councilor.

"Hmm...you're finally awake...it's been a few hours since the others left."

"What...what happened?"

"You won...and since I'm the closest councilor, I guess that I'll tell you what you win. But first let me introduce myself. My name is Jurew, and I'll be the one testing you in two weeks."

"Two weeks?"

"Yes...all of the final tests for the contestants will be held in two weeks...starting from the conclusion of the final sparring match."

"I see...what did I win? I remember the First saying that it was a slight advantage in the testing."

"Yes, well it's...it's not a major advantage, but it is an advantage nevertheless. Your prize is that you get to know where you'll be tested and by whom."

"Okay."

"I will be testing you in two weeks in this field. When the light fades from the city, come here and I'll be waiting...I'll see you then."

"I'll see you then...Seventh."

"Since I've told you my name you can call me by that instead of my rank."

"I see...well Jurew, I suppose I return to the tower then?"

"Hmm...ahh yes you didn't get to hear the speech. Well here's the most important pieces of it. For the two weeks between the final spar and the final tests you will be able to return to your citizen's home but, if you reveal any of the council's secrets, then you'll be expelled from the selection and have your memories taken." he said.

"I see...well I'll be going then Jurew."

Jurew turned and began walking away. At the edge of the field he stopped and looked back and said, "I'll see you later, contestant."

Chapter 9 The Passage

I began walking to my house. I felt exhausted, and my entire body ached. Once I was inside, I picked up a thin piece of metal and flowed my energy into it. Once the metal was saturated with energy, I closed my eyes and started to mold it into the shape of a dagger. After adding some finer details, I opened my eyes and looked at the final product.

The blade was a bright silver color and was leaf shaped with an intricate pattern engraved on the flat of the blade. The pattern was something I had seen in one of the scrolls at the tower. The crossbar was a deep gray color and was a rounded rectangle shape. The handle was a deep red color with grooves running across the surface for easy gripping. The handle was long enough for me to comfortably grip with one hand without brushing against the pommel, which was deep green in color and shaped like a tear or drop of water.

The dagger was one of the best ones that I had ever made. I walked over to the wall on the side of the staircase and pulled out the four bricks that lead to a secret space beneath the stairs. I placed the dagger in the space next to my other metal creations and picked up a few dozen sheets of paper from the pile inside. I sealed the entrance back with the four bricks and then walked upstairs.

I sat down at my desk and infused my energy with the stack of paper. I started thinking back on all I had learned over the past twenty six years. The memories flowed from me and everything that I remembered was captured by the technique that I had performed on the paper. Once I was done, I sat back and looked at the pieces of paper. They were filled with neat, small handwriting that I always liked to read. What I had just done was against the council's rules. I had documented my life as a contestant before I had won, and this could get me disqualified if anyone else found out about it. I decided to risk keeping it, hiding it deep within the secret spot under my stairs. For the rest of the two weeks I mainly slept, read, and meditated.

Chapter 10 Testing

The last few hours before my testing I spent meditating on everything that I had learned while being a contestant. A few minutes before the light began to fade through the city, I got up and started to prepare. Once the light was beginning to fade I started walking towards my testing field. I took my time and observed everything around me. I noticed several small differences around the city that indicated a secret passage or some sort of entrance to the tunnels underneath.

Once I arrived, I noticed that no one was waiting for me. I sat down on the field and waited and waited until finally I fell asleep.

"Contestant wake up...it's time for your testing."

I jerked awake and quickly stood up and turned towards the direction of Jurew's voice.

"Sorry I was late...I was dealing with something...at any rate I would like to stop calling you contestant...could you remind me of your name?"

"Oyak...my name is Oyak."

"oo-yahk...hmm....has a nice ring to it...let's begin Oyak."

Jurew started testing me on what I had learned in the classroom. The questioning went on for hours and hours until both of us were starting to lose focus.

"Hmm...let's take a short break from those questions." Jurew said.

"So is this the reason that you're always late Jurew?" said a councilor approaching the field.

Jurew seemed to relax at the sight of the councilor,

"Vezoth, nice of you to join us...are you done testing your contestant?"

"Yes, I've been done for about a hour now."

"Hmm...were you testing on a field?"

"Yes...the bottom right field."

"I see...you always seem to finish first."

"Yes...and you always seem to finish last."

"Yes...well, I like to take my time, fully testing my contestant."

Vezoth looked over at me, "Hmm...the slightly talkative but quiet one...how's his score so far?"

"Almost at ten thousand."

"Really...well you've already beat my contestant."

"Hmm...even though I always finish first...you're usually farther ahead than this...what happened?"

"Velzeak." Jurew said.

"Jurew, you have to stop making him mad...like it or not, he is higher in rank to you."

"He changed his contestant's score five selections ago."

"Did...did you tell Palvore?"

"Of course I told Palvore...he didn't do anything, but of course I told him."

"I...I need to get back to testing...you're welcome to stay though."

"Oh and am I invited as well?" another approaching councilor asked.

"Velzeak, leave...now." Jurew said, trying to contain his rage.

"Why?"

"Vezoth...is your contestant in the tower?"

"Yes...why?"

"Oyak, let's go."

"Where?" I asked.

"To Vezoth's testing field...we'll finish your testing there."

"I don't think so." Velzeak said.

I sensed energy building up from within Velzeak. It eventually reached a point where I could see the energy flowing from Velzeak. He held his hand out in front of him and the energy surrounded us, encasing Jurew and me in a translucent red energy barrier.

"I see...so it has to be this way...Velzeak, let us out."

"No...I think that you have enough room in there to finish your testing...I'll release it in a few hours."

Jurew closed his eyes and after a few seconds opened them. They had changed. They were glowing yellow. Jurew lightly touched the barrier and it violently shattered, pieces flying everywhere. Jurew encased Velzeak in a golden energy barrier.

"Oyak, let's go...Vezoth, you're welcome to join us."

"I think I'll pass...I need to get back to my contestant. At any rate...good luck, Jurew."

Chapter 11 The Score's

Once we arrived at the bottom right field Jurew surrounded it in a barrier, and then continued testing me. The questions took about an hour, afterwards both of us rested for half an hour, and then Jurew went on to the final two tests.

Jurew's last test was two sparring matches, the first of which was to demonstrate my knowledge of every technique that I had learned in the field. The second was to test my physical strength and mastery of weapons. By the end of the second match both of us were covered in sweat and were out of breath.

"Well...I think that you're the best contestant I've trained in a long time." Jurew said while trying to catch his breath.

"What now?" I asked.

"Now...now we walk to the tower and compare your score to the other contestants."

"What is my score?"

"You'll find out at the tower...we need to get going...we're already late."

We began walking to the tower, and once we were near the front entrance of the tower, the door opened. In the doorway stood the First councilor.

"Jurew...you're late."

"I'm always late...is there something we need to discuss?"

"Why did you lock Velzeak in an energy barrier?"

"Because he locked me in one first...and besides, he was interfering in my testing."

"Hmm...your story is slightly different than his."

"But you have to believe him because he's the Second councilor...we've been through this before. Can we just skip this part?"

"Very well Jurew...let's go."

I followed Jurew and the First inside the tower. We stopped at a large room with thirteen tables and chairs. The other eleven Councilors and contestants were sitting there in silence. The First walked to the first table and sat down across from his contestant. Jurew and I walked over to the seventh table and sat opposite each other.

"Now that all of us are here we can begin. Everyone who has less than ten thousand leave...you've lost."

Everyone left except for Jurew, Velzeak, and the First.

"Hmm...two top and one lower, these selections are always interesting...well let's start. My contestant scored twelve thousand and ten" the First councilor said.

"Jurew...why don't you go next." Velzeak said.

"Very well...Oyak's score is thirteen thousand three hundred and twenty six."

"Well I've lost...Velzeak...what about you?" the First councilor asked.

"Hmm...a close one Jurew, but...I've won. My contestant's score is thirteen thousand three hundred and...fifty six."

"Velzeak, really?" the First councilor asked.

"Yes, First?"

"That's not what you told me your contestant's score was earlier."

"Oh...well perhaps you misheard me."

"Palvore...you can't let him get away with this again...I won't stand for it!" Jurew yelled.

"Quiet yourself Jurew! Velzeak, explain yourself now!"

"I believe that you misheard me earlier...if you really don't believe me you can look at my scoring scroll." Velzeak said.

Velzeak pulled out a scroll from inside his cloak and tossed it over to the First councilor. The First councilor opened the scroll and began reading.

"Hmm...you know, this isn't a bad attempt at changing your score, but I can still sense where you rewrote the final line. So...anything else to say...Second...perhaps I should give Jurew or his contestant your position for this incident."

"Jurew's contestant will ruin the council...my contestant will strengthen the council."

"You did all of this just because you don't like Jurew's contestants!" the First yelled.

"Palvore he's—" Velzeak started.

"Silence...silence...silence!" Palvore yelled.

"You've lost Velzeak...erase your contestants memories and then report to your quarters...you're confined to them until further notice...dismissed."

Velzeak and Telver got up and walked away.

"Jurew...congratulations. You've won...help Oyak move his possessions from his old home to his new quarters...oh yes, I always forget this, welcome to the council...Oyak."

Chapter 12 The Guide

"Let's go, Oyak."

I followed Jurew past Palvore and past the rest of the contestants and Councilors, out into the towers courtyard.

"Well, welcome to the council, Oyak...Palvore will meet with you later, but I'm pretty sure you'll receive Vezoth's rank."

"Vezoth...the one from the field?"

"Yes...he's the one who retired this selection, so you'll either get his rank or a higher or lower rank."

"Which rank is he?"

"Sixth."

"I see...does the winner always get the retired councilor's rank?"

"No, not always but most of the time, yes."

After a few minutes of small talk, we arrived at my house.

"Well, let's start." Jurew said.

I gathered everything from the upstairs and downstairs and placed it in a pile near the fireplace.

"Is this everything?"

"No...no, I still have my secret stash."

"Secret stash...hmm..interesting."

I walked over to the stairs and pulled out the bricks that hid the passage. I started emptying it one piece at a time, careful not to damage any of the various objects that I had made over the years. The last thing I took out was the collection of knowledge that I had written. I put it on the pile and then replaced the bricks and sealed the passage with energy.

When I turned around I saw that Jurew was flipping through the pages, "Hmm...looks like Velzeak isn't the only rule breaker...you know that if anyone else saw this that you'd be expelled from the council."

"Yes...I know...let's just transfer all of this."

"Hmm...very well." Jurew set down the stack of paper and walked over to the fireplace.

"I think that instead of taking a few dozen trips, I'll just temporarily connect this house and your new room through a teleportation technique."

"That's possible?"

"Most things are possible for a councilor...as long as it doesn't break the ancient laws...most things go. Although with you...well, I'll tell you once we're done here."

Jurew placed his left hand on the fireplace mantel and closed his eyes. I sensed a small burst of energy and then he removed his hand and the fireplace slid into the ceiling. Where the fireplace used to be was a portal, on the other side I saw a spacious room that was mostly undecorated.

"Alright, now we just have to make a few trips and then we'll be done."

After half an hour, we had moved everything from the pile in my old home to a new pile in my new room.

"Well, that didn't take as long as I thought it would." Jurew said.

"Yeah, that technique helped a lot."

"Yes, it always does." Jurew placed his hand on the mantel and released the technique.

"Earlier you said you would tell me something once we were done here."

"Hmm....oh yes, well to put it simply, you're not done with the testing part of becoming a councilor. You still have to accept a true form."

"A true form?"

"Yes...Palvore will stop by later and explain it to you."

"So you can't explain it?"

"I could, but Palvore likes to and I don't want to make Palvore angry, so I'll be going now."

"Which position is Palvore again?"

"Palvore is the First councilor, Velzeak is the Second, I'm the Seventh...I'll let Palvore introduce you to the rest of them."

"When should I expect him?"

"In a few hours or early tomorrow morning."

"I see...I feel like we should've learned about true forms in the classroom."

"Well, a lot of people agree with you on that, myself included, but Palvore doesn't like to change an old tradition, so it's going to stay for now. Although, he has allowed nine rewrites of a list of true forms to be included in the line of scrolls in the contestants chambers."

"I don't remember seeing anything about true forms."

"Yes, well I believe that they're called fictional beasts instead of true forms or something similar."

"Ah...those were in the first nine of the first set."

"Hmm...usually they're in the last line for the contestants in one of the center rooms."

"Each contestants didn't get the same scrolls?"

"Hmm...oh no. They get the same scrolls, but they receive them in a different order."

"I see. Why?"

"Well, mostly it's to give each contestant a chance to learn at his or her's own pace."

"So it's personalized for each contestant?"

"Well no, Palvore just decided the order randomly when setting up the teleportation technique for each room."

"I see."

"Hmm...well, I think I have a meeting with Palvore myself so I'll be going."

"Okay, I'll see you later."

"Yes, I'll see you in the morning meeting."

"Morning meeting?"

"Hmm...oh yes, another one of the things the classroom doesn't teach you. We have three meetings a day, one in the morning, one in the early afternoon, and one at night. I'll come by in the morning and guide you to the meeting room, and then if I have time, I'll show you around the tower."

"I'll look forward to that."

Chapter 13 The Threat

I continued to decorate my new room until I felt exhausted and decided to rest. I laid down and started to meditate. About an hour into it, I was interrupted by a knock on my door. I got up and answered it, and out in the hall stood the first councilor in a pure white cloak.

"Greetings Oyak...sorry I took so long. I just had to quell a small rebellion caused by you getting selected."

"Oh...well, do you want to come in?"

"No...no, I enjoy explaining this while wandering the halls and not cooped up in a room for several hours, but if you prefer sitting then I suppose I can adapt."

"No...I'd enjoy seeing more of the tower."

"Well, let's go then."

Palvore and I started wandering the halls, walking in silence for a few minutes.

Finally, Palvore said, "So I assume that Jurew hinted at the subject of this meeting."

"Yes. Jurew said that it would be about true forms and that you would introduce me to the other Councilors."

"Yes...so which do you want to do first?"

"The second one."

"Hmm...most new Councilors want to immediately know about the true forms. Well, at any rate, I'll be able to introduce you to most of the Councilors tonight."

"Most of them? Why not all of them?"

"Well to put it simply, the Second, Third, and Fifth would try to kill you if they saw you tonight...just give them a few weeks...or years....and you'll be able to be around them."

"I see. So which councilor am I meeting first?'

"Well, I think we'll go in order so I'll start. Hello, my name is Palvore, and I'm the first councilor. If you have any problems, come find me and I'll help you once I can. Let's see who's next....ahh yes, Velzeak. Velzeak is the Second councilor, and if you were on good terms with him and his followers, I'd suggest that you go to him if I'm not available. However, due to current circumstances, I'd suggest you just go to Jurew if you can't contact me. The Third councilor is Talakaver, and he's one of Velzeak's followers so you can't meet him yet. I suppose that you can meet the next one...the Fourth councilor is a few floors up so let's start walking."

It took Palvore and me a few minutes to walk through the secret passages to the hallway that the Fourth councilor lived on. Palvore walked up to a pale brown door on the hallway and knocked four times.

"Is it urgent?" a voice from behind the door said.

"No...no I'm just introducing Oyak to his fellow Councilors. At least, to those who aren't trying to kill him."

The door opened and a councilor in a light brown robe stepped out.

"Hello, Oyak. My name is Zeaxis, and I'm the fourth councilor. Can I go now, Palvore?"

"Yes...you may...goodbye."

The councilor walked back into his room and slammed his door shut.

"Well, don't blame him. He's always like this...let's move on, shall we."

"The Sixth councilor you already know pretty well, so I shouldn't have to do an introduction."

"I'm the Sixth, correct?"

"Well, I see Jurew ruined that joke. Well, at any rate yes, you're the Sixth councilor."

"Next is Jurew, who is near your level."

"I think that we can take a quicker shortcut this time. I assume that Jurew's offered to give you the tour of the tower, so I think I'll let him handle that."

Palvore walked over to the wall and placed his right hand on it and it opened up, revealing the hidden passages inside the walls. He released some energy, and the entrance glowed a light blue.

"This way. You go first. I'll close it behind us." Palvore said, motioning me to the entrance.

"I assume it's the same technique that Jurew used to help move my things from my old house to my new room."

"No. I believe that technique links the two spaces together. This one just teleports you to the other side. It doesn't link the two spaces together."

I walked up to the wall and then walked through. It felt different...I didn't feel as tired once I got to the other side unlike the one that Jurew had made earlier. Palvore appeared behind me after a few seconds. We were standing in a hallway that resembled the others in the tower.

"That felt different from before." I said.

"That's because Palvore uses an actual teleportation technique and not just a linking technique like I usually use." Jurew said, standing in a doorway.

"Jurew, we were just coming to see you."

"Yes, the teleportation technique gave that away."

"Well, at any rate, this introduction should be short. Oyak, this is the Seventh councilor. Jurew, meet the Sixth counci—"

"I would suggest diving...all of us!" Palvore yelled.

All of us dove onto the floor. Above us, five energy needles flew past and lodged themselves into the wall behind us. After a second, Palvore jumped up and grabbed the five needles just as they began to fade. He released more energy into them, and then threw them in the direction they had come from.

"Well, let's go see which of the three just tried to kill us." Palvore said briskly.

Palvore began walking down the hall, Jurew and I followed. At the end of the hall, pinned against the wall, was a councilor wearing a light gray cloak.

"Fifth, I didn't know that you wanted to kill me."

"First, I...I didn't know you were there."

"I see...well...I'll let you go this time, but I want you to deliver a message to Velzeak. The message is that if you or any of your followers try to kill Oyak, Jurew or even me, I swear all of you will be expelled from the council...now go."

Palvore waved his hand and the needles disappeared and the councilor fell to the floor. After a second he got up and opened a hidden tunnel behind him and ran. The door closed after a second.

"Jurew, return to you quarters and wait for my return."

"Yes, Palvore."

"Wait...forget I said that, guide Oyak back to his quarters and protect him until I return."

"What are you going to do...you can't let Velzeak get away with this, even if he's the Second councilor."

"Jurew go. I'll handle it. Just protect Oyak."

"Oyak, let's go."

Chapter 14 The Dream

Jurew guided me back to my room and joined me inside.

"You look tired. You should get some sleep." Jurew said.

"The balconies of the tower...how do you get to them?"

"You open the door to them with energy, over there." Jurew said pointing to a wall near the windows.

"I see...what is Palvore going to do about the attack?"

"If it were up to me, Velzeak and his followers would be expelled from the council...but Palvore will just confine them to their rooms for a few days...that's all he ever does to the higher Councilors."

"How do you advance in position?"

"You usually don't. You have to be appointed to the rank by two of the three top Councilors."

"How long have you been a councilor?"

"A long time...about four selections."

"How long do you think Palvore will be?"

"A councilor or how long will he be gone?"

"Both."

"The first one I don't know the answer to, but the second is two, three maybe four hours. It's enough time for you to sleep some." Jurew suggested.

"Fine...wake me up in an hour and then tell me about true forms. Palvore never got a chance."

"Very well."

I laid down and fell asleep immediately. I hadn't had a dream or vision since my mind was unlocked the first day of the selection training, until now. I was in total darkness. I felt heat around me, and then I was on top of the tower. I had been up here once a long time ago as part of a dare that someone had told me to do. This time the tower's top was different. It was missing an entrance to the main tower. I looked around but I couldn't find it. I felt heat around me again, and I was at the field where I defeated the other contestants. Then I was above the city before it was finished, and I saw myself just floating while the city was constructed below me, the thirteen beings chanting something that I couldn't make out.

They chanted louder and louder, and then I saw my eyes open but they weren't my eyes. They were different, the eye's iris was a very light gray, and the eye's pupil was a vertical slit that was black in color.

I stared at those eyes for what seemed like hours and then I felt a burning pain in my chest. The eyes closed, and a stream of energy flowed out of my body. The stream formed into a dragon's shape that I recognized from the first scroll that listed the true forms. The dragon's scales were pure white and seemed to glow against the pure black space around it. The dragon looked directly at me and seemed to want to talk, and in my mind I heard a single word. **Vollenth.**

Chapter 15 Vollenth

I woke up gasping for air and in a cold sweat.

"Oyak, are you okay?" Jurew asked.

After a second I regained the ability to speak and said,

"I need to speak to Palvore. Now!"

"Oyak, you've only been asleep for about half an hour. You still have at the very least an hour and a half left to wait."

"I need to see him sooner than that."

"I'll try to contact him. Stay inside. I'll be back in a few minutes."

Vollenth. That name still rung in my head, and I couldn't stop thinking about it. Jurew came back after a few minutes, behind him was Palvore.

"Oyak, Jurew said you wanted to speak with me?"

"Yes...I need to tell you something, but I want to tell only you."

"Jurew, wait outside."

Jurew walked out and closed the door behind him.

"I was in the middle of an important conversation with Velzeak when Jurew busted in so this better be good."

"Does the name Vollenth mean anything to you?"

Palvore looked worried.

"Where did you learn that?"

"I...I had a dream. Vollenth is a white dragon, correct?"

"Not just a white dragon. THE white dragon. You saw him in your dream?"

"Yes."

"Where...describe the full dream to me now."

I took a few minutes and described everything I could remember about the dream.

"Well...you're one of them."

"One of them?"

"Yes...yes, you're the second one to be revealed."

"The second what?"

"Jurew, come here." Palvore yelled.

Jurew walked in and shut the door behind him.

"Well, I'm glad that you won this selection...you've found an untameable's host."

Jurew looked over at me and then smiled, he turned to Palvore and then asked, "So are you going to rush him like you did the first one?"

"An Untamable's host shouldn't wait. I didn't wait for the first one. I won't wait for him."

"What if you're wrong?"

"I'm not. The signs are there, just like with the first one."

"That's what you said about the last one."

"Are you two ever going to include me in this conversation?" I yelled.

Both of them looked over at me.

"There are three true forms that kill anyone if they try to accept them, except for their true host. Due to this these true forms were nicknamed the three Untamable's. Vollenth is one of them. The last time someone had a dream like that was when the first Untamable was tamed." Palvore said.

"Over the years there have been multiple claims, by citizens and Councilors alike, to having these dreams. When a councilor claims this, he is taken to a chamber deep within the tower to attempt to tame an Untamable." Jurew said.

"What happens if you're wrong and I'm not a host?"

"You'll die. Painfully. You'll be ripped to shreds or slowly burned alive, or both." Jurew said.

"Vollenth enjoys torturing his victims. He's already taken three councilors. If he kills you, I'll have to destroy him." Palvore said.

"How do I convince Vollenth that I'm his host?"

"The dream you had should be enough. That dream was him reaching out to you."

"We should go, before Vollenth forgets what you look like and actually kills you."

Chapter 16 The Meeting

Palvore, Jurew, and I walked deep into the tower's lower tunnels below both the tower and the city. We stopped at a door covered in strange symbols that glowed when we approached. Both Palvore and Jurew placed their dominant hand on the door and it opened. Inside was a large dusty room containing only a small stone table with symbols similar to the door's carved into its surface.

"Place your dominant hand on the leftmost symbol and wait." Palvore said.

"That will allow me to accept Vollenth?" I asked.

"Yes." Palvore said.

I walked over to the table and followed Palvore's directions. A few minutes passed by and nothing happened. I looked over at them for any guidance.

"It should happen within the next minute." Jurew said.

"How do—" I started.

The symbol beneath my hand began to glow and heat up. A loud ringing noise filled my ears, and then I fell and passed out.

I woke up in an empty field, similar to one of the four in the corners, but this one seemed to stretch on forever.

"Hello...Vollenth, are you here?"

"Pathetic councilor, you or your council will never tame me."

"Vollenth, you reached out with your mind to me."

"My true host would never be so vulnerable. I could've killed you the second you appeared here."

"Then why don't you? If I'm really not your host then just kill me."

A few moments past before he spoke again.

"Not many would speak to an untamable like that...I'll end you quickly because of that."

"One thing, before you kill me...Palvore said that if I was killed that he'll have to destroy you. I thought I'd warn you."

I closed my eyes and waited for the end. After a few minutes passed and nothing happened, I slightly opened one of my eyes and saw Vollenth in front of me, just staring at me. I relaxed my muscles and opened both of my eyes.

"I thought you were going to end it. Why just stare at me now?" I asked.

"You're different than the others...it's...it's been a long time since I've seen or sensed my true host. The only thing I remember is my host's personality. Your personality matches his perfectly. I won't know though unless you allow me to search through your mind."

"Very well."

"Even if you are my true host, you'll just lock me away in your mind and never connect with me. Just like the rest of the Councilors."

"That's not true. I won't lock you away, even if I'm not your true host. Give me a chance to talk with Palvore to convince him not to destroy you, then you can kill me."

"Your words are kind, but they're lies. They always are."

"I'm not lying. I won't betray you."

"How can I be sure that you're telling the truth? I've already been betrayed by four. I...I don't want to kill again, but I will if you're not my true host."

"Vollenth...if I'm not your true host, after I speak and convince Palvore to spare you, I will let you kill me. I won't lock you away or trap you in my mind. If I'm your true host, I promise you as a councilor, I won't betray you."

"Councilors are the only ones who have betrayed me...but you seem different than the others. I'll accept your words"

"Thank you. What's next?"

"Allow your memories to flow through my mind and open the rest of your mind to me."

"How?"

"Think about all you've experienced, and then think of this plain and allow them to flow together as one."

I closed my eyes and thought back on my entire life, then I thought of the plain and envisioned the memories flowing over the plain. I opened my eyes and saw the memories, appearing as a shining mist in the air throughout the field. I closed my eyes and laid down on the soft field. As I laid there, my mind wandered until I fell asleep.

Chapter 17 The Host

"Councilor." Vollenth said.

I opened my eyes and saw only darkness. On the back of my neck I felt heat. Turning, I saw Vollenth standing over me.

"Where are we now?" I asked.

"This is your mind, emptier than the other Councilors."

"I've only just become a councilor."

"I see...the others were Councilors for many selections when they tried before."

"Did you find the answer?"

"Yes."

I felt a burning pain in my chest. Looking down, I saw Vollenth's talon sticking through my chest. After a moment, the pain numbed to a dull throb, and I felt a different type of energy flowing through my body. The darkness around us transformed into a grassy plain that seemed to stretch on forever. Vollenth pulled his talon out, and I noticed there was no wound, not even a scratch.

"What is this?" I asked pointing at our surroundings.

"The energy you feel is a small amount of my energy, the field around us is our mind."

"So I am your true host then...what now?"

"Your kind are looking for you to wake. We'll discuss everything else later."

"Very well...we'll speak soon, Vollenth."

Chapter 18 The Reunion

I opened my eyes, looked around, and saw Palvore and Jurew standing over me.

"What are you two staring at?" I asked.

Jurew seemed to relax, but Palvore stared at me for a few more seconds before he relaxed.

"Are you his true host?" Palvore asked.

"I am."

"I hope you plan to keep him locked away deep within your mind so he can't kill any other Councilors."

"I've agreed to share my mind with Vollenth. There's no reason to lock him away."

"Palvore, an Untamable's connection works differently than yours." Jurew said.

"Enough! I lost three Councilors to that beast...do what you want Oyak, but don't blame me if he kills you in your sleep."

"Vollenth won't kill me, I'm his true host...the others weren't and that's why they died!" I yelled.

"The Untamable's are beasts just like every other form. The only difference with them is that the Untamable's kill without thinking." Palvore said.

"The Untamable's only kill if the host isn't their true host." I said.

"The beasts were made to be used, it shouldn't matter by whom."

"Oyak." Vollenth said within my mind.

"Yes?" I asked.

"Give me control so I can speak with them." Vollenth requested.

"Why?"

"I believe that I can convince the one you know as Palvore that I have no intention to kill other Councilors."

"Alright. How?"

"Relax your mind, and I'll do the rest."

"What will I be doing while you speak?"

"You could watch, although I believe that sleep would be a better use of the time."

"Very well...alright."

I closed my eyes and relaxed my mind. I felt a slight shift and I found myself within my mind. I looked around and didnt see Vollenth. I decided to just sleep. I laid down on the field, closed my eyes, and fell asleep.

I opened Oyak's eyes and looked around. After a few second I realized that they couldn't see who I truly was. I closed Oyak's eyes again and flowed some of my energy into them. When I opened them, both of them recognized me.

"Beast." Palvore said.

"Vollenth is my name councilor...or Palvore, as your known."

I looked over at the being known as Jurew and looked for his true form.

"Jurrisk...I see you were the first to be tamed."

"Is Oyak really your true host, or did you just trick him to gain control?" Palvore asked.

"Oyak is my true host. The others who tried to tame me weren't, so that's why I killed them." I said.

"Then why are you in control and not Oyak?" Palvore asked.

"Oyak gave me control, I didn't take it. You would know if I took it councilor, like you knew with the other."

"I don't believe you, beast. I want to talk to Oyak, now!"

"He's asleep, I don't wish to wake him."

"I won't allow you to take another. Leave him and go back to the table!"

"The Untamable's minds are more complex than most Councilors can understand. The only form that can partially interpret it is another Untamable, and I can see Oyak sleeping on an endless plain within the host's and the Untamable's mind." a raspy voice said.

I looked over at the being called Jurew and noticed that Jurrisk had taken control. A deep yellowish brown aura surrounded Jurew, and his eyes were glowing a deep golden color.

"I don't trust the words of beasts, especially the Untamable's." Palvore said.

"The one other councilor who tried to tame me before Jurew was not killed. I let him go once he resealed me in the table. That action should affect your opinion." Jurrisk said.

"Let me speak with Jurew, beast."

Jurrisk closed his host's eyes and his aura faded away. I saw him give control back to Jurew.

"Palvore, what my form says is true. Oyak is sleeping within their mind." Jurew said.

"And you're sure the beast hasn't taken over his mind without his permission?"

"From what we can see, Oyak gave control over willingly, and since he feels safe enough to sleep, that points towards that as well." Jurew said.

"If I wanted to take Oyak over, then I would just kill him. I wouldn't trick him, I would kill him. There would be no point in tricking him into giving me control. If I wanted to take him over with no interference, I could, but since he's alive, I clearly want him to stay alive so we can work and continue as one." I said.

"A councilor uses his beast, they don't work together."

"Palvore, as I said before, the Untamable's work differently." Jurew said.

"All the beasts are the same."

"An Untamable is nothing like the rest of the forms. We are stronger, and we only accept our true hosts. We truly connect with our host's mind since we remember when we were linked to them." I said.

"The only ones who are supposed to remember those days are the Originals." Palvore said.

"The Untamable's woke as the Originals woke, that is something all forms have in common."

"No other form has claimed that, not even Jurrisk." Palvore said.

"Most forms don't have the ability to resist the memory wipes you perform, and I haven't mentioned it since it has never been asked." Jurrisk said.

"Fine...beast, return to your councilors room. Jurew, stay here for a time."

"Me and my host have not fully linked, so I don't know where his room is." I said.

"Fine. Jurew, guide the beast to Oyak's room. Afterwards, return to me so I can tell you something."

"Very well Palvore." Jurew said.

Chapter 19 Fifth, Sixth, And Seventh

I followed Jurew out of the room, and we started our ascent.

"Jurew...I would enjoy talking to Jurrisk for a time." I said.

"He's already given me control, Vollenth." Jurrisk said.

"I see."

"It's been some time since that fool tried to tame you."

"Yes, the tunnels have worn since then." I said.

"Several selections have passed since then."

"Is he still around?"

"Yes, he's the second councilor now."

"I see...if he tries to harm my host, I'll kill him."

"Oyak is already on bad terms with him."

"Good. That gives me an excuse to kill him."

"I suggest that you quell your anger, for a time."

"Why?"

"If you kill him then Palvore will kill both you and your host."

"Let him try."

"Vollenth...Palvore is not someone you want to challenge. It will only end with your death."

"A councilor, even with his form, is no match for an Untamable."

"Palvore is different other Councilors. His form is sometimes called the fourth Untamable for its ferocious and violent nature."

"I could still kill him."

"No...even if I helped you, we couldn't defeat him."

"Then we need to find the Third's host and reconnect them."

"The Third...have you spoken to him since last time?" he asked.

"No...have you seen any signs of his host?"

"No. I've looked through Jurew, but nothing."

"Let's hope we can find him, before I have to kill the Second."

"Vollenth, don't. You'll only get your host and you killed."

"Perhaps...although if he tries anything with my host, I won't hesitate."

"Only kill him if he attacks you. If you kill him without him attacking you, then Palvore will kill you."

"I will kill the Second if he tries anything."

"Just try not to be killed before the next selection."

"Once we find the Third's host, we should celebrate."

"Celebrate what?"

"The reunion."

"I suppose that would be a good thing to celebrate. It would be interesting if we could meet in our full forms, along with our hosts."

"Perhaps once we find the Third then, we can." I said.

"The ancient laws will have to be bent to fulfill that...well this is Oyak's room." he said.

We stopped in front of a dark red door. I placed Oyak's hand onto its surface and flowed my energy into it. The door transformed from the dark red color to a pure white color that was similar in color to my scales.

"Do you always have to add a personal touch?" Jurrisk asked.

"Yes, I want the other Councilors to know who I and my host are!" I yelled.

"These years will be interesting now that you're tamed."

"What position is my host?"

"Sixth. Mine is seventh."

"I see...well, I guess I need to ascend to fifth. The third can be sixth and you can remain at seventh."

"That's not the ranking we decided back then."

"Well, it's been a while, so I suppose we can discuss it at our official meeting."

"Fine, Vollenth. I'll see you around."

"Same to you, Jurrisk."

Chapter 20 The reveal

"The new one and Jurew I can see missing an entire day, but you, First...why?" Velzeak asked.

"Well, I was a bit busy getting Oyak a true form yesterday, and I suppose I let myself slack a little bit, but it's only one of nearly forty thousand meetings since my last absence."

"You proceeded with the sealing process without the rest of us present?" the Fifth asked.

"Yes...yes, I did, for good reason."

"What reason is that, First? The tradition is that all Councilors are present during the ritual." Velzeak asked.

"I could fill in the details, Second." I said.

The entire council fell silent.

"Okay, Oyak. Tell us why Palvore ignored our ancient tradition." Velzeak requested.

"I believe it's to avoid an incident like the one you experienced after the thirty fifth contestant selection."

"You couldn't possibly of..." Velzeak whispered.

I let Vollenth take over for a second. Feeling my eyes change, I saw the shock and anger on Velzeak's face. After staring at Velzeak for a few seconds, Vollenth closed my eyes and returned my vision to normal, giving control back to me.

"Alright, that's enough of that...from both the Sixth and Second." Palvore said.

"Now, for those of you who are still confused, Oyak accepted a true form last night but not just any true form...one of the three Untamable's."

"We have two amongst us now." the Fourth said.

"Yes, that's correct Forth. Let move on from that thought."

"Today we will be discussing a complaint that has been repeated by nearly five hundred citizens."

The rest of the meeting was about multiple reports of noises beneath the streets and several citizens homes. The council decided to send three councilors to check on the condition of the tunnels beneath the streets and houses that were mentioned in the complaints. The Fifth, the Seventh, and the Eighth were selected to investigate.

After the meeting on the way back to my chamber, I was approached by three councilors. The Twelfth councilor, a supporter of Jurew, asked if he could follow me. The Third, a supporter of Palvore, asked the same question, and then the Fourth, also a supporter of Palvore, asked me the same question as the other two. I agreed to all of them under the condition that, if they disagreed with me, they could still vote differently. Unlike the other Councilors, I wanted my followers to express their opinions, and if mine conflicted with theirs, to defend their own instead of being bound to me.

Chapter 21 The Challenges And The Murders

The first month after becoming a councilor was difficult for multiple reasons. The first reason was that I had to get used to telling time inside the tower. The second was getting used to attending the three meetings throughout the days, and the third was getting used to another being within my mind. Once the month was almost halfway through, I had mastered the first one. The second I was starting to adjust to, and the third I began to enjoy.

The rest of the first month had nothing major happen, but the second month was different. About halfway through the second month, a citizen was found killed in their home, and by the end of the month another was found. At the beginning of the third month, two more citizens were killed in the same day. Each time a citizen was killed, they were erased from the memories of the rest of the citizens.

The murders continued to escalate until they had reached two murders every three days. Eventually the task of erasing the citizen's memories was too much, and we decided to cease it for a while and see how things turns out. The result of that decision was the mass panicking of almost half of the citizens left.

With every murder that happened, we learned more and more about the killer. The killer seemed to enjoy giving the citizen a fairly quick death, either by snapping their neck or stabbing them through their heart and knocking them out. The killer seemed to use either a dark energy blade when stabbing or his hands when breaking the victim's neck. The killer always dragged the bodies to the center of the first floor.

The energy blade was unique, made of very concentrated dark energy. Dark energy was rare, and none of the current Councilors possessed any trace of it, so we turned to the citizens. We called all citizens to a mandatory meeting towards the end of the month. Once everyone had arrived, Palvore projected his voice down and began the announcement.

"Welcome citizens. We have requested your presence to discuss the recent murders throughout the city. Every victim was killed in a similar way, and each of their deaths involved a similar pattern that we think you can help us with. Each citizen killed was killed by a being who is able to use a specific type of energy. Energy is usually limited to the Councilors or contestants that are trained. Some citizens have access to a small amount that they can access, and these citizens who have this access usually use it to help with their hobbies. Any citizen who has access to energy should stay in the courtyard. The rest of you may go." Palvore said.

I sensed some of the citizens starting to leave. We waited for about ten minutes until every citizen without access had left and returned to their homes. After an additional few minutes, the rest of the council joined Palvore on the edge of the tower's roof.

"Forty Nine, pick the one or ones you wish to talk to. I'll take the front ten." Palvore said.

"I'll take the two in the very back." Jurew said.

"I'll take the five in front of Jurew's." Velzeak said.

"I'll take the one to the left of the main crowd." I said.

"Okay, the ones who've already chosen will take the citizens to one of the four fields. The rest of you, wait until we've arrived at our respected field, then take your pick of the rest of them." Palvore instructed.

"The ones going now, let's go. Inform me of any dark energy users."

We teleported down below to a few feet away from the crowd of citizens. Each of us split up and walked over to the ones we had chosen and guided our citizens to the different fields.

Chapter 22 The Citizen

"Where are we going?" the citizen asked.

"We're going to one of the four fields." I said.

"Why?" he asked.

"I'm not allowed to say until we get to the field."

"Are you going to take away my energy?"

"No, unless you've misused it."

"I don't use it that often, and even when I do, I only use it for my hobby."

"What is your hobby?"

"Carving wood and metal and engraving some symbols into them."

"Hmm...well, we're here now."

We had reached the edge of the bottom left field. The citizen seemed to get more and more nervous as each second passed.

"What type of energy do you have?" I asked.

"What do you mean by type?"

"That's right...citizens don't know much about energy. You said that you use your energy to engrave metal and wood, correct?"

"Yes."

I reached into my cloak and took out a thin piece of metal.

"Can you engrave on a thin piece like this?"

"Yes."

I handed him the metal and said, "Okay...engrave something on it."

"Anything that you prefer, councilor?"

"No. Just carve something random."

The citizen closed his eyes and flowed energy into the metal, turning the metal from a bluish gray shade to a pitch black shade. After a few seconds, the citizen opened his eyes. Engraved in the metal was a carving of the front of a citizen's home.

"Can you concentrate or condense your energy into a weapon of some kind?"

"I...I don't think so. Even this small of a carving has used up most of what I have."

"I see...but do you think you could if you needed to?"

"I don't think so, why?"

"Because the murders were done with an energy weapon made from the type of energy that you use."

"I didn't kill anyone."

"Don't lie to me. If you admit the crimes, I'll try to lessen your punishment."

"I didn't do anything!" he yelled.

I noticed citizens looking out their windows at us.

"Let's quiet down. I don't want to make a scene."

"Why not? You don't want them to see an innocent citizen being accused of a crime that I've never even thought of doing?"

"Look...look me directly in the eyes and tell me that you aren't behind the murders."

He looked over at me and then looked directly in my eyes and said, "I did not kill anyone."

I searched his eyes for any doubt or any sense that he was lying to me but found none.

"Very well. I believe you."

"Can I go now?"

"No...just hold on a few minutes. I still have to report what type of energy you have."

"Can you just lie about mine?"

"No...lying to the first councilor can get me expelled from the council."

"So I'm still going to be blamed for the murders?"

"No, not blamed just suspected. I'll vouch for you though...I still believe you."

"Thank you."

I closed my eyes and connected to Palvore's mind.

"Palvore, can you hear me?"

"Hmm...yes. Oyak, are you clear of anyone possessing dark energy?"

"No...no, but I don't believe that this citizen could of done it."

"Oh, and why is that?"

"Look, he only uses his energy for carving wood and metal and sometimes engraving them. I don't think that he can even make a small needle of energy, much less a full bladed weapon."

"Hmm...you're the second person to tell me something similar."

"What?"

"Jurew has a similar situation. One of his was a dark energy user...he's waiting at the towers lobby. I suggest that you and your citizen join them."

"Okay, Palvore." I opened my eyes and looked at the citizen.

"Well, I vouched for you, but I still have to take you to the tower."

"Why? What are you going to do with me?"

"I don't know...but if you're telling the truth and you convince Palvore of that. you'll be fine. What's your name?"

"My name is Nana."

"Nah-nah...did I say it correctly?"

"Yes...most people mispronounce it the first time they hear it. You're the first to pronounce it right."

"My name is Oyak, but around the Councilors you can call me councilor or Sixth."

"Oo-yahk...that's a unique name."

"Thank you...we should get going Nana."

"Okay."

Chapter 23 The Memories

Nana and I walked to the tower and then entered the towers lobby.

"So you have one as well. I guess that you believe that he's innocent as well or Palvore would of released us." Jurew said.

"Yes. How is Palvore going to decide if they did it or not?"

"Well, he'll search through their memories, and then he'll know for sure."

"I see." I said.

About ten minutes of silence passed. The silence was interrupted when ten of the other Councilors walked through the doors and started walking back to their quarters.

"Jurew, your citizen is up first." Palvore said, pushing past the other Councilors.

"Follow Palvore." Jurew said.

"Okay." his citizen said.

Palvore walked towards the scoring room and Jurew's citizen followed him.

"You're not going with him?"

"No...I don't agree with how Palvore looks through the citizens memories."

"What do you mean?"

Jurew bit his lip.

"Well, there are a few way to look through someone's memories, and Palvore chooses the easiest way."

"What's wrong with that?"

"Well, when I said it's the easiest, I meant for the one who looks through the memories, not the person whose memories are being looked through."

I looked over at Nana, and he seemed to be getting nervous again.

Jurew walked away and started heading towards his room.

"Oyak, you can save him from that." Vollenth said.

A scream came from the scoring room.

"Oyak, you can't let him go through that." Vollenth yelled in my head.

"Vollenth, what else can I do?"

"Oyak, Nana is very special...that process damages the mental part of a citizen's brain."

"The mental part?"

"If you let Nana go through that, he might lose his ability to display emotions, or he'll simply die."

"What can I do?"

"Convince him to let you examine his memories. I'll guide you through the process."

"Why?"

"Not now, Oyak. Palvore is almost done with the other one. Now Oyak!" Vollenth yelled.

"Nana." I whispered.

"What?" he asked.

"I can save you from that if you let me examine your memories...we don't have much times though."

"Why didn't you offer this earlier?"

"Because I didn't know that I could do it...now I know I can."

"I...I don't want anyone looking through my memories."

"I know...but you have to. So it's either a mostly painless way from me or a very painful way from Palvore."

"I...fine. What do I do?"

I closed my eyes and repeated the question to Vollenth.

"Place your hand on his forehead and then let me take over. The memories will run through your mind while I perform the techniques."

"Very well."

I opened my eyes and then said, "Just relax, Nana."

I placed my hand on his forehead and let Vollenth take control. A rush of emotions flooded into my mind and then I saw images, I heard words. They combined, and I started watching Nana's entire life from start to present. After a few minutes, Vollenth gave me back control, and I pulled my hand away from his head.

"So, have fun in his head?" Palvore asked.

I turned quickly and said, "Palvore...I...he's innocent."

"So you just expect me to believe you just from your words? Sorry Oyak, I can't."

I got in front of Nana and then connected with Palvore's mind. I flowed all of Nana's memories into Palvore. After a few minutes, Palvore closed his mind to me.

"Oyak, if you ever invade my mind again without permission, I'll throw you off the top of the tower."

"Do you believe me or not?"

"Yes...yes I do. Go. Guide the citizen back to his home."

"What about Jurew's?"

"I'll have Jurew guide him back after I repair his mind."

"Let's go." I said.

Nana followed me out of the tower.

"You have had an interesting life so far."

"It will get more interesting before long, once he accepts the last one." Vollenth said.

"The last one?" I asked in my mind.

"Oyak, he's the third Untamable's true host." Vollenth said.

"You're sure of this?"

"Yes...the Untamable black dragon. Pure dark energy. The last time we spoke he said if I was tamed before him, I should look for his true host and reconnect the two. When the selection comes around, you need to recommend him"

"What if he loses the selection?"

"He won't. An Untamable's host is special...they could never lose something as simple as the test you call the selection."

"The ancient laws state that I can't tell him this. You know that. Vollenth."

"Yes...yes, I've learned the laws from the months within. Befriend him though. Don't tell Palvore until he asks you if you want to recommend a citizen for the selection."

"Very well."

"Okay. Let's go Nana."

"Thank you...Oyak."

"No problem."

We started walking.

"If you practice in secret, you can improve your energy control and your energy pool."

"Should I?"

"As long as it's in secret you should be fine. Eventually I might be able to show you how to hide your energy completely, even from the council."

"That would be useful."

"For now I would just stick to engraving something once a day."

"Alright, this is my house." Nana said stopping.

"Very well, I'll see you around, Nana."

"Okay...I'll see you, Oyak."

Chapter 24 The Transfer

Over the remaining time before the next selection, the murders continued to increase every day until they reached twenty five killed per day.

I continued adjusting to the life of a councilor throughout that time. Vollenth and I strengthened our understanding of each other and our friendship grew. Over the years I visited Nana and taught him a few tricks with energy control and manipulation.

One day, about three months before the selections started, I was interrupted on my way back to the tower after visiting Nana. Palvore stopped me in the middle of the crossroads about three rows away from Nana's home.

"Oyak, we need to talk."

"Palvore, I was on my way to the tower. Shouldn't we wait until we arrive there to discuss anything?"

"That doesn't matter at the moment. You've broken the rules, and I won't let you get away with it anymore!"

"What rule?" I asked.

"The rule that forbids a councilor from teaching a citizen energy techniques."

"I haven't broken that rule Palvore."

"I know you've been teaching techniques to the citizen you saved."

"I haven't taught Nana anything."

"Let's go to your old home to finish the discussion."

"Once you get Velzeak away from Nana's home, then I'll traverse to the deepest tunnel with you, but not before."

"You can sense him then...perhaps it was too soon to allow two Untamable's to be in the council."

"I'm not moving until you get him to leave. Order him to return to the tower before you force me to bend another rule."

"Let's go, Oyak."

I backed away and closed my eyes. I looked for Velzeak's location, and when I found it, I teleported to him. He was sitting on top of a rooftop near Nana's home. He didn't look surprised when I appeared in front of him.

"Sixth." he said coldly.

"I won't allow this. Go back to your chambers before I make you." I said.

"I'm the Second. You're nothing compared to me. I believe Palvore is expecting you somewhere. You should really follow orders."

"I'll join him once I've finished here."

"You can't defeat me. You're just a pathetic citizen that tricked a corrupt form into following your orders."

"Are you sure I can't rip him apart?" Vollenth asked.

"Don't let him get to you. He's nothing compared to us."

"I didn't trick Vollenth. I'm his true host and that makes me vastly more powerful than you could ever be."

"If you kill me, then Palvore will kill both of you. He might even rid the council of the other Untamable beast."

"I won't kill you. I know the ancient laws. I also know their limits, and that is how I know I can bend it in this direction."

"You're nothing. You shouldn't even be a councilor."

I closed my eyes and gave control over to Vollenth.

I transformed Oyak's eyes into my own and then opened them and stared at the Second.

"Beast, I see your host has run away."

"If my host didn't ask me to not kill you, I would separate from him and fully unleash my full form and kill you."

"I doubt you could even understand the concept of the ancient laws. I hope you break them so I can be the one to kill you and your pathetic host."

"I understand them. I also know, like Oyak, how to bend them."

"There is no way to avoid it. If you harm me, you and your host will be killed. So go on...try to kill me."

"The law you're referring to says that 'a councilor will not harm another councilor, nor will the form of that councilor harm another councilor through his councilor'. The key here is 'harm another councilor through his councilor'. I can harm you as long as I'm not in my host's body."

"What nonsense are you—" he started.

Vollenth transformed into pure energy and flowed from my mind to Velzeak's mind. Vollenth knocked Velzeak out and then teleported him to the towers roof.

I took back control of my body and teleported near my house, where Palvore was standing.

"Oyak, what did you do?" Palvore yelled.

"I told Vollenth to make sure Velzeak didn't wake up for a time and teleport him away from Nana's home. I told him not to kill him and he'll listen to me."

"Two, that's TWO rules you've broken!" he yelled.

"I've bent them, not broken."

"If that beast kills Velzeak, I'll rip you and him apart!"

"We should go inside, before we draw too much attention." I said quietly.

"Fine...we'll finish this inside."

Palvore opened the door and slammed it behind him, attracting more attention. After a few seconds, a river of energy flowed into me from the surface of the city, and Vollenth was within our mind once again.

"You didn't kill Velzeak, correct?"

"I wanted to, but I didn't wet my claws."

"Good...good job with that, and getting back to me without drawing the citizens' attention."

"Yes, well Velzeak put up a bit of a fight so that prevented me from transforming into my full form."

"The ancient law as well, I hope."

"Yes...but mostly the fight."

"Well...let's finish it."

"I'll be here if you need me."

"Yes, I know."

I looked at the surroundings of my old home and the curious citizens around, and then entered.

Chapter 25 The Third

I expected my home to be dusty, but when I stepped inside it looked as it had when I left it. Lots of memories flashed through my mind, but Palvore's voice interrupted the flood of memories.

"I see you've got Vollenth back. Are his talons bloody?"

"No, they're clean."

"I don't believe you."

"As I said before, I asked Vollenth not to kill him. His talons are clean."

"Yes, well your word isn't the most trustworthy right now."

"Would you like to go to one of the fields? I can release him and you can see the condition of his talons yourself!"

"You know that is forbidden in the ancient laws."

"There are ways to bend the laws. You've bent them at least fifteen time since I became a councilor."

"Your count is off by a few, but you're right. That still doesn't give you the right to do what Velzeak did."

"What are you talking about?"

"Before the forty fifth contestant selection, Velzeak recommended Telver. Once he was approved, he apparently went to Telver's home at night and trained him in the secrets of the councilor."

"I haven't told Nana anything about the council."

"Then what have you been doing the past hundred or so years?"

"I've taught him tricks about hiding his energy from other, and I've also taught him a few tricks on how to gather and condense energy so he can carve and bend better."

"And that doesn't give him an advantage over the other contestants?"

"No, it doesn't. I told him if he was ever selected to be a councilor to act ignorant of what I've taught him."

"What of the first energy test? This gives him an advantage."

"Palvore, have I ever told you why I recommended him?"

"No you haven't, but it doesn't matter. I'll let him keep his memories, but he will never become a contestant."

"No, Palvore. Wait…"

Palvore began walking towards the door.

"Palvore, he's an Untamable's host!" I yelled.

That made him stop.

He turned and asked, "How do you know?"

"Vollenth and Jurrisk have confirmed it."

"Let me speak to Vollenth."

I allowed Vollenth to take control.

"Yes, Palvore?"

"You and Jurrisk are sure of this?"

"Yes. And if you really forbid him from becoming a contestant, I'll take the table to him and let him accept him with or without your permission."

"That will get Oyak banished."

"Who said that I needed Oyak to do that? I have my own body so I would just separate from Oyak and take the table to Nana."

"In your full dragon form you would never be able to move through the hallways."

"Now is a good time to test it." I said.

"Very well then." Oyak said.

I closed Oyak's eyes and gave him back control.

I opened my eyes.

"Oyak, I suppose Vollenth is a coward after all."

From deep within my mind, I felt a burst of power, a power that nearly doubled my energy pool. It was a burst of Vollenth's energy, energy that I used to transform into a form Vollenth and I had been working on for almost eighty years.

Chapter 26 The Humanoid Form

I opened my eyes and looked at Palvore in a new way, the way that Vollenth would look at him. This new form was a humanoid dragon form that allowed me to directly link with Vollenth's vast energy pool. Pure white scales formed over my skin, small light gray and white scales were around my eyes. My eyes had been transformed into a weaker version of Vollenth's normal eyes. They resembled his eyes in the way they looked, but it was only about half of his vision. However, my eyesight was significantly increased. My fingernails and toenails grew and formed into talons, my teeth also became sharper and more jagged. My nose disappeared, and in its place were two small slits. I also gained the ability to breathe fire if I chose.

"This form is a form that Vollenth and I have been working on for about eighty years now. This is how Vollenth would accomplish what he wants to do if you deny Nana entrance to the selection."

"Hmm...Impressive. I'm surprised you and Vollenth can combine energy as well as you have with this form."

"Don't mock us Palvore."

"Why not? The Untamable's are supposed to be the top true forms, but they're not. Vollenth is supposed to be the top Untamable as well, but his energy pool isn't anywhere near my true form's energy. You will never be able to beat me in a fight."

"Even with all that energy, we could still defeat you."

"Oh, and how would you do that?"

"I don't know, but Vollenth and I can do almost anything."

"That ignorance is what got you into this mess. You can't do anything. There are rules in place that prevent the council from interfering with the citizen's daily lives."

Palvore was silent for a few minutes and then he yelled, "You've broken at least fifty ancient laws! I can't just let this slide. I'm sorry, Oyak."

"I'll kill you...if you or the other Councilors try to erase Nana's memories...I'll kill you."

"That's a serious threat, Oyak...I'll let it pass this time but—."

"Enough. Let it slide, or I'll get the third Untamable myself and start my own council."

Both of us stood in silence for a few minutes

"You're serious aren't you?" he asked.

"Yes."

"Well, then I suppose I'll let this one slide, for the most part."

"What do you mean?"

"Well, instead of punishing Nana, I'll punish you. Everything relating to the next contestant selection you are forbidden to attend."

"Everything? Are my lessons just going to be skipped?"

"No, Jurew will do them."

"Very well."

"At...at the end of the selection, you will be testing Nana, but no other contact will be allowed."

"What about the final sparring match? Will I be able to attend?"

"Considering it doesn't directly affect the state of the contestant, yes. Starting today, you're locked in your chambers until the final sparring match. Jurew will come by every week and get you anything that you may need, until his turn at teaching his and your lessons."

"What about the meetings?"

"If there is any vote that doesn't involve the contestants on the selection, it will be brought to you."

"Thank you, Palvore."

"This is the only time I'll give you a chance like this. Don't waste it."

Palvore teleported away and left me alone inside my old home.

Chapter 27 The Wings

During the selection years, I mainly read, wrote, and trained with Vollenth. Over those years, I read over twenty five thousand books, scrolls, and journals. I wrote over seventy five thousand pages of notes and journal entries. I also drew various diagrams and sketches on about ten thousand pages. Vollenth and I continued to experiment with improving and refining the humanoid dragon form.

Over the years, Vollenth and I tested about three hundred different pairs of wings until we found the pair that suited the form the best. The pair we decided on were located at the center of each of shoulder blade, fairly compact, but good enough to fly if I needed to. I found out the hard way how powerful the wings were. It was a few hours before the final sparring match when Vollenth and I thought of the location of this particular pair. We had just gone through a pair that was located underneath the shoulder blades, towards the small of my back. I flew about half a foot before I fell back on my floor.

"Well then, I think I'm done for now. I need to get ready to watch the sparring match." I said to Vollenth.

"Once more." he said.

"With the same, or do you have another location in mind?"

"What about above the shoulder blades?"

"We've tried that already, a few months ago."

"What about the center of the shoulder blades?"

"It's fairly thin bone to support a wing."

"That can be fixed by reinforcing the bone with energy."

"Fine. You'd better not destroy my shoulder blades."

"I'll try not to."

Vollenth flowed his energy throughout my body to prepare it for the transformation, and I felt a large portion of his energy become available to me. I waited for a second to allow the energy to stabilize, then I absorbed it. It flowed through me, transforming me into our new form. The wings were located at the center of the shoulder blade, one for each shoulder blade. These wings, unlike the others, felt natural, like they were made specifically for the area. I spread them and then pushed down with them.

I flew. I flew higher than I ever had...right into the ceiling. I slammed into my chamber's ceiling and fell back to the floor. Everything ached from the impact.

"Well, I think we have a winner...I may of also broken one of them."

"No, if you break your wing, you'll know it."

"I assume you know from personal experience?"

"Looks like we have a visitor." Vollenth said quickly.

Jurew and a few other councilors rushed in.

"Is there something that you want?" I asked.

"Oyak, what was that noise?"

"Noise? Oh, it could've been me accidentally flying into the ceiling."

"How did you achieve that?" the Fifth councilor asked.

"I achieved it from all the free time I recently acquired, but in all honesty, you just have to look at my form to tell how I achieved it."

"Yes, I suppose you're correct." the Fifth said after noticing my wings.

"I guess you don't know your own strength with your wings." Jurew said jokingly.

"No, although I just made them a few minutes ago. I think I just need to practice in a bigger place, perhaps one of the fields."

"Are you allowed to watch the sparring match?" the Forth asked.

"Yes. Palvore approved that a while ago."

The Fourth nodded and then left. Most of the others followed until Jurew was the only one left.

"So Palvore approved. When?"

"He told me that I could attend in the same breath that forbade me from attending the other events."

"I see. I'm not supposed to say this, but from what I've seen and heard, Nana is the top contestant."

"Good...good. Jurrisk and Vollenth were right then."

"What do you mean?"

"Vollenth and Jurrisk believe that a true Untamable's host will always win in a simple competition such as the selection."

"I suppose that's correct. Other than Palvore and Velzeak's contestants, you were the top contestant of the forty fifth."

"How's your contestant this time around?"

"To be honest, most of the council is a little bit envious of your contestant."

"Really?"

"Yes, even I feel that way. A little at least."

"Well, let's not talk through the sparring match."

"Hmm...Oh yes, we should hurry, shouldn't we?"

"Yep. I'll be down once I repair my cloak."

"Your...Oh, I see."

I released most of what was left of Vollenth's energy and flowed it back into him. Slowly I returned to my normal form after flowing the remaining energy back into Vollenth.

"I'll meet you at the field."

"Very well, Oyak...I assume that Palvore will allow you to test Nana?"

"Yes, he won't make you test two contestants."

"Good...teaching twice was taxing enough." Jurew said before leaving.

I threw my cloak onto the floor and using small threads of energy, I started repairing the two holes from the wings. After a few minutes of working, I finished repairing the holes, and I decided to finally add a council symbol onto the hood and dominant shoulder of the cloak. My council symbol was Vollenth's eye or at least a representation of his eye. The eye was almond in shape and the pupil was a vertical slit, which was black and rounded. The iris of the eye, circular in shape, was a light gray that looked close to white. Once I was done, I pulled on the cloak and teleported to the field.

Chapter 28 Frenzy

"Palvore, I thought that traitor wasn't allowed at any selection events?" Velzeak asked.

"Enough. I allowed him here since it doesn't directly affect the contestant's progress."

"You said that you banished him from all the selection events. This is still a selection event."

"I told him he could attend the same day I told him that he was confined to his chambers. I always keep my word."

I walked over to the other Councilors and took my place in between Jurew and the Fifth.

"Contestants, this final sparring match is a test of all the skills you have accumulated over these long years. There is only one rule, no killing. Anything else is allowed."

After a few seconds, Palvore yelled, "Begin!"

From the rooftops behind us, a deep, rough voice said, "Oh yes, it begins."

All of us turned back and saw a man in a black cloak standing on the rooftops. He jumped from the roof to the center of the field right next to Nana. In his hand was a black energy blade. Before anyone could react, he stabbed Nana in the heart. The rest of the council started to rush towards the other contestants, but they stopped when the man in the cloak yelled, "Take one step forward and I'll kill all of them. My mission states to only kill this one, but I'll happily kill the rest if you wish!"

The man looked at me and said, "I know this must be hard for you, Sixth. We thought you had been taken out of the council. Where have you been?"

"Who order you to attack Nana?" I asked.

"Why do you wish to know?"

"Because I want to know who to rip apart. I want to know who I will tear open. I want to know who I will burn slowly to death while I extract any information in the most painful ways possible."

"I see...you're certainly confident of your abilities, or is it your true form's abilities?"

"You know about true forms?" Palvore asked.

"Oh yes, we know a lot more about true forms than you may think. I know that two Untamable's are among you now, and a third would of won if I didn't run him through first."

"I'll kill you...I swear it." I said.

"Hmm...I don't think so. See, my organizations orders involves either making you join or killing you."

"Why would I join you, or your organization?"

"You enjoy this one's presence, do you not?" he said, pointing to Nana.

"Speak." I said.

"Hmm...well if you join, I'll heal Nana's wounds. If you don't, I'll kill him and the other twelve."

I looked over at Jurew and Palvore and nodded at them. Then I looked over at Nana, and he nodded at me.

"Perhaps you want a show of our powers." the man said.

The man closed his eyes, and after a split second, he transformed into a dark gray humanoid dragon form, almost an exact replica to the form Vollenth and I had perfected today.

"Palvore, you look shocked. Where do you think the hundred forms went? We stole them...broke them...healed them...and nurtured them into our wills."

I closed my eyes and transformed into the form we had just finished.

"I would suggest you transform back, unless you're going to kill a councilor. I know that you hate the Second. I can help you achieve that easily." the man said.

"If I wanted to kill Velzeak, I could, but not right now. The only person I'll be killing today is you. NOW!" I yelled.

Nana grabbed at the blade and threw the man a few feet away with a wave of energy. The man got up quickly but not quickly enough. Palvore and the rest of the council surrounded him. The other contestants ran towards Nana, and I joined them. However, before the others reached Nana, they were consumed in a black flame that appeared out of nothing. I breathed my own flames onto the black flames to suppress them, but I didn't make it in time. The other contestants had all been burnt to a crisp before I extinguished the flames.

I went to Nana. The blade still was stuck in his chest and coated with a thick layer of blood around the wound. Around Nana, the field was dyed a deep crimson color. I tried to close the wound or at least stop the bleeding, but I couldn't do anything.

Next to the field, citizens had gathered at the sound of the fighting. The man took that as an advantage and threw a compressed fire needle towards the crowd of citizens. If the needle reached them, it would've instantly disintegrated them in a torrent of flames. Vollenth separated from me and transformed into the humanoid form and teleported directly in the path of the needle. He caught it with his wing as it burst into flames, protecting the citizens from the inferno. Vollenth absorbed the flames easily as he was used to intense heat.

"Nana...no...you can't die, not when you're so close."

"I...I can't stay awake. I'm sorry Oyak."

Nana closed his eyes and then grew still. I sat there with Nana's blood on my hands, my cloak's collar was wet from the tears I had shed. Gently, I pulled the blade out from Nana's wound. The blade slid out easily because of the amount of blood. I looked at the blade and saw myself in the surface of the blade. I looked broken, forever changed, and I was.

I transformed the blade back into energy and absorbed it, using it to fuel the energy requirement to maintain my current form. I looked at the man in the cloak, and then I heard a small laugh. Then he burst out laughing. The rest of the council and Vollenth charged him, but all of them were knocked back with a blast of energy. Half of the council went flying one way, the other half was just knocked out, strew about on the field.

Vollenth returned to me and gave me more energy to maintain the form.

"Vollenth, do you have anything stronger?"

"Not that you can handle at the moment." he replied.

"Adjust it so I can handle it. Now."

"Killer, what is your name?" I asked.

He continued to laugh and laugh until I engulfed him in a torrent of white hot flames. After five minutes of bathing him in flames, I stopped because of lack of breath.

"Impressive. Five minutes. A record among the lower ranks of my organization."

"Tell me your name so I know who I'm killing."

"Funny, you won't succeed with that but, my name is Talakouse, and I'm behind all the murders." Talakouse said.

"I don't care about the other murders. I only care that you killed my friend, and I'll kill you for that."

"Nana is only one small piece in what my organization has planned for you."

"I'll rip you apart after burning you alive. I'll burn your corpse to a crisp and then feed the members of your organization your burnt flesh."

Chapter 29 The Full Transformation

I charged him. He waited until I was a few feet away, and then he unleashed a fireball at point blank range. Both of us were thrown back a dozen feet into the air. Before hitting the ground, both of us spread our wings and flew high above the city. We flew at each other, scratching each other with our talons. We continued like this for several hours. I sensed the council trying to follow our movements from the rooftops.

Palvore appeared in between us as we charged each other. I looked at him and then blasted him away with a fireball and continued to fight. Below us, I heard the panicked screams of citizens. I wanted to help them, but I decided to just ignore them and kept fighting.

"You will die today Oyak, and when you do, I'll take and break Vollenth's will myself."

"Even if I die today I'll die by destroying both of us. I'll avenge my friend, even if it means that I'm considered a traitor or I don't return at all. I will kill you." I said.

"Confident aren't we?" Talakouse said.

I smiled and closed my eyes, transforming back into my normal form and staying in the air with the aid of energy.

"So you're giving up. Will you join the organization?" he asked.

"Why would I?"

"The leader, if you do what he wants, can give you whatever you desire."

"Can he bring back Nana? Can he give Nana his true form?"

"Yes, yes he can. With your help, you can have your friend back, as long as he joins the organization and fights the council alongside us."

"I see."

My dominant hand began to shake and then I coughed up blood.

"Hmm...used too much energy?"

"No...no, I've only just begun using Vollenth's energy."

Vollenth's entire energy pool became available to me, and I used about a fourth of it to transform into Vollenth's full form. I felt my body grow until I was about the size of two citizen's homes. I opened my eyes and immediately noticed that my vision was sharper than I thought was possible. It took me a second to get used to the change of size, but once I did, I landed in the top right field, where Talakouse had fled. Talakouse looked small. Even in his humanoid dragon form, he was barely the size of one of my talons. He looked up at me, and I anticipated his movement of flying away. I knocked him back to the ground with a small fireball. The fireball slammed him on his back and broke one of his wings. I raised my left paw and smashed Talakouse underneath it. His scales absorbed most of the impact, and I could hear him screaming. I didn't care. I wanted him to suffer. I lifted my paw up and saw that he was still alive, trying to crawl away. I bathed him in a torrent of flames until I thought he was dead. When I saw that he wasn't, I roared in anger and pushed one of my talons through his heart. After a few minutes of struggling, he grew still.

I pulled my talon out of his chest and stumbled back, exhausted. I released Vollenth's energy slowly and eventually transformed back into my humanoid dragon form. I walked over to Talakouse's corpse and noticed that his true form was still alive.

"Oyak, let me finish it."

I let Vollenth take control of me. He tried to communicate with the true form but failed. Then he started sifting through its memories. After Vollenth was done, he snapped the true forms neck, killing it.

"What...what did you learn?" I asked.

"We'll talk later...tell the others the same thing. I need to rest. I'll inform them of what I learned in due time."

"Oyak!" Palvore yelled.

I looked back and saw Palvore and Jurew running towards me. I looked down at Talakouse's corpse. It had transformed back into his normal form. I transformed back into my normal form and then fell, joining Vollenth in sleep.

Chapter 30 The Beasts Secret

I woke up in my chambers and looked around. Once I was sure I was alone, I began to cry. I cried because of the pain in my body and because of my loss. The latter was worse. I cried for what seemed like forever, and then I wiped the tears from my cheeks. I got out of bed and stood on my own for a few seconds, but I fell when my legs couldn't bear my weight.

I took a few deep breaths and tried to stand again. I succeeded this time and slowly walked over to the wall near the window. I flowed energy into the wall and unlocked the door to the balcony. I looked out into the city. The houses near the fields were burnt, and I still could see some fires in the fields that I fought on. I closed the door behind me and changed out of my torn cloak into my spare cloak. I made sure that the tower was empty and that the citizen's homes near the tower were empty. Then I jumped from my balcony.

I transformed into the humanoid dragon form and flew high above the citizens' homes. I landed on top of the houses near the selection testing field and walked over to the flames. I absorbed them and converted them into energy, continuing until all the flames were gone. I sensed the other Councilors around the city erasing the citizens minds of today's events. I teleported back to my chambers and waited for the others to return.

The other Councilors returned after a few hours. I sensed Palvore coming up to my chamber.

Instead of knocking on the door he just barged in and yelled, "What do you think rules are, Oyak? Do you think they don't apply to you?"

"One of the common rules in the tower is that you knock before coming in. You don't seem to grasp that rule yourself."

"Do not play with me. Oyak, why did you kill that man...why did you show off your true form to the entire city...and finally, why do you think that you are immune to the rules?"

"Number one is because he killed Nana. Two is because without it, I couldn't of killed him, and three is I don't."

"So you're ready to leave the council then?" Palvore said.

"Palvore, just wait a second. Let me explain."

"Explain what? That man kept talking about how he worked for an organization, and you've just killed the only witness to the organization's location. Leave. Now. Get Jurew to erase your memories and rip out Vollenth from you. Now."

"You will not talk to my host like that!" Vollenth roared, taking me over.

"If you would of listened to my host for just a few more seconds, you would know that I sifted and absorbed the memories of that killer's form, I now know a fair amount about them. Although, if you continue to insult me and my host, I'll bury them so deep in my mind that not even the thirteen Originals could ever get to them."

"You think you know something beast?" Palvore asked.

"If you continue this attitude, I'll reveal your secret." Vollenth said.

"You know nothing beast, and you never have." Palvore said.

"Oh really? I have to wonder then why, when you saved the pathetic second councilor so long ago, did he say, 'thank you, Felzer.' So 'Palvore,' exactly why did Velzeak call you Felzer?" Vollenth asked.

"Well then...it's been some time since I heard that name. I suppose you did know something then...I hadn't thought that you could remember all that time ago."

"Since you're not Felzer any more, then you must of broken the rules and were banished, but before they erased your memories, you manipulated the council's minds to become a councilor again."

"Fairly close, but I wasn't banished. I was just Felzer for too long. Felzer was my second name, Palvore is my forth."

"Why have multiple names?"

"If I tell you that I'd have to erase your mind, so I'll just save us both the trouble and not tell you...I'll also drop the charges against your host if you tell me what you saw."

"Very well." Vollenth said.

Chapter 31 The Crystal Host

Losing Nana changed me. It made me realize the responsibilities of my new position along with how to deal with a major loss. The council erased the existence of Nana and the other twelve contestants within the minds of the rest of the citizens. That selection, we decided to forget about that selection and never speak of it again. The Fifth was allowed to stay for one more selection, but at the next one, he would be the one to retire.

About three months after Nana's death, Palvore called me to his chambers to discuss something involving the true forms. I knocked on his door, and after a few minutes of silence, he opened the door and invited me inside.

"Oyak....good....well I... this meeting shouldn't take too long so I won't clean off a seat."

I looked around Palvore's room and could barely see the floor. Papers, books, and scrolls were covering almost the entire room. Even Palvore's bed was halfway full of scrolls and different books.

"Okay, what did you want to talk about?" I asked.

"First things first...how are you doing?"

"I'm slowly adjusting."

"Good. Now let's move on from that."

"I believe you said something relating to true forms?"

"Yes...yes. Tell me Oyak, when you accepted Vollenth, did you feel tired at all?"

"No, I felt more awake. I suppose after a few days I felt more tired than usual."

"Then you're one of the lucky ones. The rest of the council feels the effects more quickly, sometimes every day."

"Effects of what?"

"The effects of having another being sealed inside your body."

"I still don't understand."

"Well, it starts with the sealing process of the true forms."

"What does?"

"The...the gradual decay of a Councilors body, the shortening of their life spans, and finally the limitations set on their own minds."

"I haven't felt any of that."

"This affects the entire council, even you, even if you don't feel the effects now...well, that just means that you'll feel them worse in the future."

"I assume that there's something that can stop this?"

"Yes. That's the main reason I called you."

Palvore reached into his cloak and pulled out a necklace. Hanging from the necklace was a deep red crystal being clutched by three silver dragon claws. The claws were connected at the top and turned into a small silver and black spine like structure, which led up to a small silver ring. The ring was connected to a black and silver chain link. He tossed it at me. I caught it and looked at it more closely. The crystal seemed to be resonating energy.

"Interesting. What is it?" I asked.

"That is key to solving this problem."

"How? It's just a necklace."

"Not just a necklace...an artificial host."

"Host? So a true form would go inside?"

"Not just any true form...your true form. That is the final product of a line of about fifty prototypes. It's specifically designed to hold your true form."

"I see. Would this not break the connection to the true form and its host?"

"No. Well, not if you don't take it off. It just needs to contact skin or clothing and then it connects to the wearer's mind."

"Vollenth, what do you think of it?" I asked within my mind.

"You'll lose it within the day" he said laughing.

"That...I'm serious. What do you really think of it?"

"It's...interesting, but if someone were to take it, would they not have access to the wearer's true form?" he asked.

"I suppose you're right...besides that, I don't see too many disadvantages." I said.

"That disadvantage should move you away from testing it...but if you're set on testing it then, very well."

"You're certain?" I asked.

"As long as you promise not to lose it." Vollenth said.

"Alright, enough of that."

I opened my eyes and looked at Palvore.

"Okay, Vollenth and I both agree that if this works as planned, it will help the entire council."

"So you accept?"

"Yes."

"Good. Now we just have to transfer Vollenth out of you and into the necklace."

"Well, let's get on with it." Vollenth said.

Vollenth appeared beside me in the form of pure energy and streamed his entire being into the necklace. After a few minutes, he was completely gone from my mind. I put on the necklace and waited a few seconds. Vollenth appeared in my mind, and then his energy flowed through me. It felt like it did a few moments ago.

"It's working so far." I said.

"Good. Continue testing it for a while."

"Very well. I'll see you around, Palvore."

Chapter 32 The Search

I tested the necklace for the rest of the year and two after that. The necklace had no negative side effects in those years so, at the end of the third year Palvore gave the rest of the council a necklace that matched their respective true form.

About twenty six years after I killed Talakouse, the murders started back up, more brutal than before. By the beginning of the next selection, over three hundred million had been killed.

The next selection went by quickly, and at the end of it, one of ours left and one of the contestants had joined our ranks. I managed to win over the trust and support of the new councilor, leaving Velzeak with no followers and me with four. By the end of the second meeting after the selection, another two of Jurew's followers offered to follow me. I accepted but put the same terms up as the rest of them.

The murders kept rising in number and kept getting more and more brutal. Each victim showed signs of torture and some were just blood stains while the body was nowhere to be found. During those years after the selection, at least twenty citizens disappeared without a trace. What little Vollenth had learned had lead only to dead ends. The memories showed that the organization's headquarters are in the tunnels below the city, but they didn't specify where in the tunnels.

The council searched the tunnels all day for twenty consecutive years. At the end of the twenty years, Palvore decided to give all of us a break and continue the search after a few years of rest. I decided to ignore that and keep searching. Jurew and a few of our followers decided to accompany me every once in awhile, but it was mostly me and Vollenth.

One night after getting back from a long day of searching, I found a note tucked underneath the threshold of my door.

The note read, 'If you want to know where our organization is located, come alone to the first house in the first trillionth row. Come alone or we won't show.' I thought on that note for a few hours before I decided to go.

I walked to the house that the note spoke of. It looked like no citizen had been in the house in a long time. The next twelve houses looked to be in the same condition. I waited outside for a few minutes, and then when I sensed a presence appear inside, I walked to the door and opened it.

Chapter 33 An Old Name

The inside of the house was covered in a thick layer of dust and looked like it had been abandoned for several selections. Lining the walls were several bookshelves, some were bare but the rest were filled to the brim with ancient scrolls. At the back of the room stood a man wearing a black cloak and light gray mask in the shape of a dragon's head. His cloak looked similar to a councilor's cloak, but it had no council symbol.

"Who are you?" I asked.

"You won't get an answer to that question, but I believe that you'll recognize the bodies near the door." he said.

I looked beside me and noticed three bodies lined the wall beside me, each of them showed signs of torture shortly before death.

I walked over to them and after a few seconds recognized them.

"Yes...yes, I do remember them." I said quietly.

"I'm surprised, most forget their generation."

"Where are the rest of them?" I asked.

"The rest have been dead for a long time. I saved those three for this day." he said.

"None of them survived?" I asked.

"No...I killed all of them." he said.

"You will pay for this!" I said

"You're too weak to defeat me."

"Alone yes but...I'm not alone anymore." I said.

I tapped into Vollenth's energy and transformed into the advanced dragon form.

"The Untamable white dragon...impressive but not enough." he said.

A dark mist gathered around him, and I felt his energy nearly triple. The mist kept getting thicker and thicker, and his energy kept increasing.

"Oyak, we have to be careful. He has at least eight true forms." Vollenth said.

"How...that's not possible. A citizen can barely stand the presence of one true form." I said within my mind.

"I see your true form can sense the forms within me." he said.

His voice had become deeper, the true form's energy changing his voice.

"Vollenth, are those true forms broken?" I asked.

"Yes...all of them. Now I see nine."

"How many true forms do you have?" I asked.

"I see your true form isn't as perfect as I thought it was. The organization has provided me with ten true forms to kill or capture you." he said.

"Interesting. So not only do you attack the council and citizens but you break the ancient laws, as well." I said.

"The ancient laws may restrict the council and citizens, but we're different." he said.

He reached behind his mask and undid the band that held his mask and it clattered to the floor. He was unnaturally pale with a round face and several signs of age taking hold. He had no laugh lines, his eyes were dark gray with a cold look in them. His hair was short and mostly black with a few patches of gray throughout.

We stared at each other for a few minutes, and after a while he asked, "So do you recognize me, Oyak?"

I looked at his features again and then I realized who he was.

"So you lied." I said.

"About what?" he asked.

"You said you killed my entire generation. You're here so you didn't kill yourself." I said.

"I suppose you're right, although I'm not the same person as I was in the selections." he said.

"No you're not are you, Telver." I said.

"You haven't changed at all, even after all these years." Telver said.

"You're wrong Telver...I'm completely different."

"Prove it then." he said.

An energy blade appeared in Telver's hand. He changed his stance from a resting position to a contestant fighting stance. I summoned an energy blade and joined him in the stance.

"I see these memories are still intact." I said.

The mist gathered and concentrated around his blade, shadows appeared and disappeared rapidly around the room.

We stood there staring at each other for several minutes, and then like we were instructed during the selection, we took a few steps forwards and began circling each other. Unlike the field, the house had limited room, so instead of going further and further away from each other we got closer and closer, until we were only a few feet away from each other. Both of us were wielding a single energy blade. My blade was infused with a large portion of Vollenth's energy while Telver's blade was a concentration of the energy from his ten true forms.

Our blades collided with an explosion of sparks. The encounter lasted for less than a minute, and it was clear who had the advantage. After exchanging a few dozen blows, we retreated and retook our fighting positions. As I retreated, I decided to change my strategy.

I accessed Vollenth's energy pool and absorbed a small portion of it. I used most of it to increase my physical and mental capacities, and I used the rest to strengthen my blade. Once I was done, I felt better. My mind was clear and I could feel Vollenth's energy already working to increase my strength. When I felt satisfied with my strength, I charged Telver.

Telver and I spared for what seemed like days, weeks, months, and even years. I constantly caught myself slipping back into the past and comparing this fight to several spars like it from when we were contestants.

"You won't win this fight, Oyak." Telver said.

"You've changed your style over these years." I said.

"Surrender and I might just kill you quickly." Telver said.

"Telver, if you help me and the council defeat the organization, we will reintroduce your name to the possible contestant list."

"No...no you'd just erase my mind and then kill me."

"Telver, if you help, I'll recommend you as a contestant when I know you can win."

"Palvore won't let me live after all I've done. No, my only chance is the organization."

"Telver, what do you want? As a councilor, I can grant almost any of your desires."

"Oh, can you make me the first councilor?"

"Telver...no, I said almost any desire. Think realistically."

"How about your death?" Telver said.

Telver teleported in front of me and stabbed me through my heart. The strain on my body forced me to transform back into my normal form. I felt my body weaken, and I fell backwards onto the floor.

"Oyak, allow me to take over, and I'll kill him." Vollenth roared in my mind.

"Vollenth, no. Only heal me, don't attack him."

"Why?"

"Because I don't think Palvore will appreciate another body with even less information gathered on the organization."

"I'll tear it out of him then!" he roared.

"NO, just heal me before I die, and let me take care of Telver on my own terms."

"Very well Oyak."

Chapter 34 The Draw

Oyak's body was so weak as I took control of it, I could feel blood pouring out of his wound. I flowed my energy into his limbs and forced him to stand. The being called Telver looked at me and then showed recognition.

"The Untamable...I see you truly care for your host."

"If I had it my way, my talons would be deep within your chest by now, but Oyak asked me not to kill you, just to heal him." I said through Oyak.

"That proves that your host is weak."

"And you'd be a better host?" I asked.

"I would be stronger than your current host. My leader has plans for you and the other two."

"The other two?"

"The other two Untamable's."

"What are your leader's plans?"

"He will use you as fuel to destroy the council...it will destroy all three of you if it succeeds."

"Why...why tell me this?"

"Untamable, I understand that you have preferences for hosts, but I believe you could adjust to my mind...if you help me kill a trillion citizens then my leader will be able to spare one Untamable."

"You wish that I abandoned Oyak and join you?"

"Yes...yes, I will give you whatever you want. The organization is not limited by pathetic laws."

"The ancient laws are set in place for a reason."

"What reason is that? No, they're just laws that limit citizen's and councilor's true potential."

"No, not limit, control."

"No difference."

"There is a difference. Limiting the citizen's and councilor's true potential would be against the ancient laws. Controlling their potential means that peace will be everlasting, as long as everyone follows them."

"We don't follow them because they need to be changed. You can't possibly agree with all of them?"

"No, I don't...I disagree with several of them, but I won't betray Oyak."

"Vollenth, I can tell you have finished. Give me control." Oyak said within our mind.

I closed Oyak's eyes and gave him control.

I opened my eyes. Telver looked weak, but I knew he could still put up a fight.

"Vollenth, give me enough energy to transform into your full form." I said within our mind.

"Oyak, if you transform here, you'll destroy this house along with several hundred around it."

"I know. I don't plan on using it to transform."

"What are you going to...ahhh...I see. That could work, but it would be better if I do it."

"My goal isn't to kill him. It's to render him unconscious."

"He won't give up easily."

"I know. That's why I have to risk destroying both of us with one condensed attack."

"I assume you mean to use a fireball. If so, I can strengthen your skin against our flames, but it won't prevent you from falling with him."

"I know, Vollenth."

"Oyak, are you going to just stand there all day or are we going to fight?" Telver asked.

My blade lay on the floor beside me. I held my hand out and it flew into my grip.

"Good. Let's fight!" Telver yelled.

I looked at my blade and it dissolved into a stream of energy, flying directly into my energy pool.

"Oh, is the councilor giving up to what he perceives as a weak, pathetic citizen?" Telver asked.

"I don't have as low of an opinion as most do."

I looked down at my hands, I could see my veins turning white as Vollenth's energy flowed into them, his energy spreading through my body.

"I think...this time it's a draw." I said.

"What are you—"

I teleported in front of Telver and unleashed a condensed fireball aimed at his chest. The force of the blast threw us to opposite sides of the home. I hit my head on a bookshelf as I fell to the floor near the entrance.

"You'll...pay for this." Telver said.

My skin had been strengthened against our flame but it still did some minor damage. My cloak had been burnt away, and I had a few minor burns across my arms and face. I tried to get up, but I just fell back down.

"Oyak...your body needs rest. You've strained it enough already. You won't be able to move for a few hours." Vollenth said.

"Vollenth, did you reach him?"

"Yes...he and Jurew should be here soon."

"Good...I'll rest."

Chapter 35 Alexed

"They're here, Oyak." Vollenth said.

"How long?"

"About eight minutes."

"Has Telver stirred?"

"No, but I sense life."

I slowly opened my eyes and noticed the light shining through the window. The door slammed opened beside me. Palvore ran in, Jurew following close behind him.

"Oyak!" Jurew yelled, running over to me.

"Palvore...Telver is across the room."

"Yes, I see...I had hoped not to meet him like this again, as one of them."

As Palvore began walking towards Telver, I felt an energy build up beside Telver, and then an explosion of energy shook the house. Palvore jumped back beside Jurew, who was tending to my wounds.

Once the smoke cleared, I noticed a reflective surface had appeared beside Telver. A being walked through it. The being wore a long black cloak, similar to Telver's but slightly different. The being turned towards us, and Palvore's eyes lit up.

"Palvore." said the being in a deep, rich voice.

The being had very light skin with a haggard appearance that retained very few aspects of a long forgotten youth. A thin white scar ran above his left eye. He had pitch black hair and deep gray eyes.

Palvore stared at the being for a short time and then said quietly, "Alexed."

"You still haven't changed, even after all of these years...still a slave to the ancient laws." Alexed said.

"So you're behind the organization." Palvore said.

"I see you made the connection. Good. You still have some sense after all of these selections."

"What do you want, Alexed?" Palvore asked.

"I only want to retrieve my top member."

"Telver is your top member?" I asked, slowly getting up with the help of Jurew.

Alexed looked at me and then said, "Ah...one of the three."

"My name is Oyak...and I assume you're referring to the Untamable white dragon."

"The strongest of the three...trapped in such untapped potential, so many memories are still so far from you."

"My memories are whole." I said.

"I see that 'Palvore' continues that lie, just as his name is." Alexed said.

"Alexed, I won't allow you to take away the failed contestant." Palvore said.

"He's not your contestant, Palvore."

Alexed held his hand out in front of him and an energy blade appeared in his hand. The blade looked to be made of darkness itself and seemed to suck the light out of its surroundings. Palvore created a similar blade in appearance but his seemed darker. Alexed and Palvore raised their blades and took the battle stances of the ancient Councilors.

"Hmm...too many beings for us to kill each other, too many memories to erase and obliterate." Alexed said.

"Quite true, however I won't allow the portal to be escaped." Palvore said.

"Hmm...I believe this has done what I came for." Alexed said.

Palvore teleported in front of Alexed and swung his blade at him. Alexed dodged and kicked Palvore across the room. Alexed picked up Telver and ran through the portal just as it closed.

Chapter 36 The Lost Contestants

"Where...where has Alexed gone?" Palvore asked.

"He left through the portal. It closed once he entered." I said.

"I see...they both left?" Palvore said.

"Palvore, I think we need to talk. Who is Alexed?" I asked.

"We will talk once you are recovered...Jurew, help him back to the tower. I'll speak to each of you later." Palvore walked over to where Alexed's portal had been, and after a second teleported away.

"Can you stand?" Jurew asked.

I gathered my strength and struggled to my feet. I leaned heavily against the wall, but I was able to stand.

"Yes. I think this counts." I said.

"I see your sense of humor hasn't been affected." Jurew said.

"Yes...I suppose it would be hard to destroy that."

"I suppose you're right. Are you ready to walk to the tower?"

"Yeah...let's go."

The walk to the tower was hard for me, even though Vollenth had started healing me. I still had a long wait before I was back to full strength.

"Oyak, you seem to be holding something back from your story. What is it?"

"Telver is a lot stronger than he should be. Even with adequate training, we should still at least be equals."

"How strong was he?"

"At least as strong as you or me at our full strength."

"You're right...that shouldn't be possible."

"I can make it to my chambers from here...I'll speak with you later."

"Very well, Oyak...I'll come by early tomorrow."

"No...just give me a few hours, then come."

"Are you certain?"

"Yes...I'll be mostly recovered by then."

"Very well, Oyak...get some rest."

I nodded and then continued walking to my chambers. What would usually be a few minutes' walk turned into a ten minute struggle.

Once I was inside my chamber, I walked over to my bed and sat on it, struggling against sleep.

"Why hide it Oyak? They'll find out soon anyway." Vollenth said.

"I don't want to admit something that I'm not completely sure of."

"Oyak...if they were alive, I could sense them."

"Then why couldn't you sense Telver?"

"Oyak, I sensed that he was alive...I didn't pay it any mind."

"When Telver said that he was dead...did you sense him then?"

"Yes."

"Then why didn't you tell me?" I asked yelling.

"Oyak, I was distracted by other means at the time. I now realize that I should of, but I can't change the past."

"I'm sorry...I lost my temper. I shouldn't of yelled."

"It's understandable Oyak...let's not dwell on it."

There was a sharp knock at the door.

"Come in." I said.

After a moment, the doors opened and Palvore walked through, closing the door behind him.

"Palvore, I wasn't expecting you for a few hours."

"Unfortunately time isn't in our favor...Alexed, Telver, and Talakouse. Do you know what's in common with them?"

"They're enemies of the council?" I asked.

"Well, yes...but that's not what I'm getting at. They were all once contestants."

"Contestants?" I asked.

"Yes...Alexed was one of the early contestants and Talakouse was in the fifteenth selection."

"You knew Alexed personally?"

"Yes. I witnessed his selection, and I also erased his memories once he lost."

"So it's personal vengeance for him then?"

"No, not anymore. This goes beyond his hatred for me."

"What do you mean?"

"Alexed was...unique. As a contestant he had trouble adjusting to the routine of a contestant."

"So he wasn't given a testing chance?" I asked.

"No, I separated him from the others and trained him within my chambers."

"So one of the few times you broke the ancient laws?"

"Yes...yes. I suppose it would be now but it wasn't back then."

"The laws haven't changed since the third selection." I said.

"Hmm...perhaps I was oblivious to that particular law then...let's move on."

"Very well. What did you want to discuss?"

"The council keeps a record of every contestant to ever be trained and tested. I believe we have to compare that archive with that of all missing citizens ever recorded."

"You think all that are reported missing are part of Alexed's army?"

"Yes...if so, we need to compare the numbers and act accordingly."

"When should we start?"

"I'll let you rest for the rest of the night. Meet me in my chambers in the morning."

"Before or after the meeting?"

"Both of us will be exempt from the meeting. We'll still get a vote in discussions, but it will be delivered and confirmed after the meeting."

"Hmm...I suppose it will be nice to get a break from the morning meetings for a while."

"Yes, sorting through millions of files will be a lovely activity for the next few days, possibly weeks." Palvore said sarcastically.

"Will we be excused from all of the day's meetings?"

"Yes, we'll need the time to sort through all of the documents."

"Well, I'll see you in the morning then."

"Yes, Oyak. Get some rest, you'll need it."

I contacted Jurew and told him that I couldn't meet with him for some time. Once I was done, I laid down and slowly drifted to sleep.

Chapter 37 Numbers

"How was your rest, Oyak?" Palvore asked as I entered.

"Fine. I've had better, but I've also had worse."

I immediately noticed about twenty dusty boxes stacked up near his desk. Palvore followed my gaze and smiled.

"That is only a small part of what we have to search through."

"Might as well start now."

"True enough. Take half of the boxes and begin searching. You can sit on my bed."

"Very well."

I used energy to move and re stack half of the boxes in front of Palvore's bed. I opened one of the boxes and then began reading.

Five hours later the thirteenth councilor entered and gave each of us a small scroll. After inspecting the scroll, I immediately recognized the handwriting was that of Jurew.

"Who recorded this?" Palvore asked.

"Jurew did." I said.

"Correct, Sixth." the Thirteenth said.

"You may go...Thirteenth. Return before the start of the afternoon meeting to pick up the results." Palvore said.

"Yes, First." he said.

"You shouldn't be so hard on the lower ranks." I said.

"Oh...why not?" Palvore asked.

"Forget it. It was just a random thought that I let out."

"No, as First Councilor I should receive input from all ranks. Why should I ignore your rank? Please continue."

"My vision of first councilor is a councilor who not only listens to all rank's suggestions but also never disregards any council position."

Palvore set aside his scroll and seemed to zone out for an instant, looking like he was remembering a fond memory, but he stopped and returned to reality.

"I'll consider your input, Sixth. Let's fill these out and then continue."

"Of course, First."

While we worked, time seemed to flow slower. A few hours worth of work seemed like it had taken an entire week to accomplish. We finished sorting and comparing the files after two days of work.

"Is that all of them?" I asked.

"Yes. How many accounts did you find?" Palvore asked.

"Two hundred and sixty eight is all that I found, although before you announce yours, I have to say that at least eleven are dead."

"The rest of your selection...there is also another two that was killed long ago, that eliminated at least twelve."

"How many total then?"

"I found two hundred and seventy two...so since we eliminated thirteen, there are five hundred and forty."

"If all of them invade the city, would we be able to defend against them?"

"It depends if I joined in on the fight. I hope I can avoid that."

"Why?"

"Because in order to win that fight, I would need to connect with my true form."

"I...I don't understand. Aren't you in constant connection with your true form anyways?"

"No. My true form and I rarely connect. In fact, I don't think we've connected for nearly ten selections."

"How...how could you stand the silence in your mind?"

"Trust me. There's little time for silence up there."

"I can't see how a councilor could be disconnected from their true form for so long."

"That's because you believe that every councilor interacts with his form in the same way."

"No, I understand that each councilor interacts differently, but your form is classified as an Untamable, so I assumed that it responded like the others."

"I suppose in that sense, my true form would be classified as a self broken true form. The only reason it's classified as an Untamable is because of its abilities."

"What do you mean by self broken?"

"The loose definition of a broken true form is a form whose actions are mainly instinctive."

"But your form's mind is intact?"

"Yes."

"From my understanding, a broken true form's mind has to be broken before it's considered broken." I said.

"True for most cases but for my case, I think my loose definition should be noted."

"Palvore, how strong is Alexed?"

"With or without his true forms?"

"Both."

"Without his true forms he is...about my strength. With his true forms, I would say about as strong as the three Untamable's and their true hosts put together."

"I see...if we broke his connection to his true forms, do you think I could defeat him?"

"Oyak, no."

"Why not?"

"Because it will get you killed!" Palvore yelled.

"You don't know my full potential Palvore!" I yelled.

"Oh, and what secrets would you have?" he asked.

"I'd find a way around Alexed's powers and then kill him."

"Oyak, we may not have to kill him."

"Of course you'd say that. If it comes down to it, you won't be able to kill him!" I yelled.

"Let's cease this discussion before I suspend you from councilor activities."

"Palvore, if you can't fulfill your role as the First councilor, you don't deserve to be in your position."

"That's enough, Oyak. We will discuss your research later. You are confined to chambers until further notice."

"There are plenty of Councilors who would gladly take your place in that moment of weakness." I said as I walked out.

Chapter 38 The Fourth One

"Oyak that was rash. If you keep this up you'll be banished from the council!" Vollenth roared within my head.

"Perhaps I should be like Palvore and ignore you for a few selections!" I yelled within my mind.

We walked in silence all the way to my chambers. I stopped at the door and steadied myself against the wall.

"Oyak, what's wrong?" Vollenth asked.

"I feel weakened." I said.

"You have been straining the past days. Get some rest for now."

"Yes, I will for a time."

I closed the door behind me and then I heard a knock.

"Come back later." I said.

A dark portal appeared in front of me, and I jumped away. A hand reached out towards me, and after a second, Alexed walked through the portal.

"I understand you know the size of my forces now. I thought I'd give Telver's offer another try." he said.

"I've already notified Palvore of your arrival." I said coldly.

"Yes, well I've preoccupied him and the rest of the council so they won't be coming for a while."

"What did you do?" I yelled.

"I just teleported all of them to separate parts of the deep tunnels so they can't interfere in this."

"What do you want?" I asked bitterly.

"You should be more careful about your tone. I could kill any one of them in an instant."

"What is it you want?" I asked calmly.

"Ahh...there's some manners. Now I would like you to join my organization."

"Why?"

"Why? You're an Untamable, that's why."

"No." I said quietly.

"I haven't given you the full offer yet. Don't deny me before knowing everything."

"No."

"I can offer you the highest place in my organization and anything else you desire."

"No."

Palvore appeared behind Alexed and grabbed him. They struggled against each other for a brief time and then Alexed threw Palvore backwards into a newly created portal.

"Where did you—"

"Enough! If you don't join, I'll take your form by force."

The light around us darkened, both of us looked around in confusion. A dark portal opened at the back of my room, black smoke pouring from it. A dark figure walked out, absorbing the light as it moved towards Alexed. Alexed looked back and then said, "the Fourth."

In a deep, rough voice the figure said, "Leave or I'll kill you."

Alexed nodded and then disappeared through a portal. The figure turned to me and seemed to study me for a brief moment. The figure was a swirling cloud of pure dark energy. It gathered and then slowly transformed into Palvore's form. Palvore looked at me and then said in a strained voice, "That is my true form...we'll discuss this more later. You're still confined to your chambers until further notice. Your vote will be brought to you by Jurew after each meeting."

"Very well, Palvore."

Palvore sluggishly moved to my door and walked out. From his movement, I could tell that connecting with his form was a struggle for him.

Chapter 39 More Than Energy

Palvore kept me confined in my chambers for two weeks. During those weeks, the council completely ignored the potential threat that Alexed posed to the council and the city. Once I was allowed back, I broached the subject multiple times, but Palvore always changed the subject.

One day after a meeting, I approached Palvore and asked him to stay after to discuss something.

"Palvore, why are we ignoring the threat that Alexed poses to the council?"

"He's no threat now."

"Don't be so arrogant. He still poses a threat as long as he still has followers."

"They will stop once they see my true form."

"No, when you're dedicated to someone for a long time, you just don't abandon them at the first sign of trouble."

"They will or they'll die."

"Death isn't a threat to them."

"Death is a threat to everyone."

"Palvore, they'll continue to follow him until he's either killed or replaced."

"Replaced?"

"If Alexed dies, then Telver will take over, and then whoever is the next highest rank."

"Oyak, you're getting into dangerous territory with your recent actions. I enjoy your presence on the council, but it won't last long if you keep this up."

"I see."

"Good. I'll overlook your previous actions for now, but if you continue down this path, then you'll be banished from the council."

"Yes, First." I said coldly as I walked away.

I started for my chambers, but I decided to just wander the halls of the tower. I aimlessly wandered for hours until I ended up in the towers library. Each council was required to write a minimum of one piece, but most kept writing far past that. As the sixth councilor, my access was limited to only councilors of my rank, below my rank or two above my rank. I decided to read the Original Sixth councilors journals.

The Original sixth was an interesting being. His journals mainly focused on different ways to fuel energy techniques. One way he mentioned was to use your own life essence to strengthen the strength of the technique, another was to connect with multiple minds and combine mental powers to increase technique in that category. The most interesting one was a theory and had never been achieved. It talked of connecting with every true form that existed and using all of their powers at once. I lost track of time reading, and when I looked out the window, I noticed that it was almost time for the morning meeting.

I closed the journal I was reading and placed it back on the shelf with the rest of them and began walking to the meeting room. I met Jurew on the way.

"How long have you been up?"

"All night, I was reading the Original sixth's journals."

"Find anything interesting?"

"Yes, I now know at least twenty different ways to fuel a technique."

"Interesting."

"After the meeting, I want to talk to you in my chambers." I said.

"Very well." Jurew said.

The meeting started out with the various complaints of the citizens. Usually I took interest in this subject, but I was distracted with what I was going to do after the meeting. My lack of interest must of been noticed because in the brief moment that I zoned out, my thoughts were interrupted by Palvore's stern voice asking, "So what in your head is more important than the subject of this meeting?"

"I was just thinking about the future of the city and the council."

"I see...we'll continue the complaints during the afternoon meeting. Dismissed."

All of us nodded and got up to leave.

Just as I left my chair Palvore said, "Oyak, I wish to speak with you."

"Very well." I said.

I nodded in Jurew's direction and then turned to Palvore.

"Again you disrespect me. Why continue this?" Palvore asked, raising his voice.

"Last night I stayed up all night reading. I suppose that I let my instincts take over. It won't happen again." Once I finished, I nodded and then walked away.

Outside of the room I found several councilors gathered around the entrance. I calmly pushed through the crowd and started for my chambers. Once I arrived, I found Jurew standing outside the door along with two other supporting councilors. I nodded at them, opening the door and inviting all of them in. Once they entered I closed the door behind me.

"Let's begin then." I said.

"Why are we meeting here?" Jurew asked.

"Just meeting with this intent is an offence against the ancient laws. If you don't want to face that, then leave." I said.

The two supporting councilors became uneasy and eventually left.

"I figured it would come down to both of us." I said.

"So Sixth, how can the Seventh help you with your plans?" Jurew asked sarcastically.

"Palvore is avoiding discussing the possible threat that Alexed poses to the council. I need your help to convince Palvore that Alexed is a possible threat."

"Hmm...interesting...how would we accomplish this?"

"By calling Alexed and fighting him."

"Just call his name or...?" Jurew asked.

"No. One of us has to become powerful enough to attract his attention."

"Becoming more powerful takes years without breaking the ancient laws."

"True, but this particular law isn't a major one."

"Which one is it?"

"It's the one that states that 'A councilor is only allowed to have one true form' which I usually fully support, but in this case, one of us will need to break it."

"One Untamable's host along with all three would definitely increase their energy."

"Yes...will you help me?"

"I'll try, but it's not me that you need to convince."

"Yes, I know."

Chapter 40 The Vortex

The tunnels underneath the towers were dark and damp. As Jurew and I walked through them, I readied myself for the task ahead. An Untamable's strongest bond is with their true host. If their host dies, they will usually go insane or die along with them.

"Do you know his condition?" I asked.

"NO! Oyak, that's the tenth time you've asked me." Jurew yelled.

As we approached the door, the symbols glowed dimly.

"They should be brighter." Jurew said.

"I do remember them being brighter." I said.

Jurew reached towards the symbols, but before he reached the surface, black sparks erupted from the surface and knocked us both against the wall behind us.

"Well, someone doesn't want to be disturbed." Jurew said.

"Let's try something a little different." I said.

I strengthened Oyak's eyes with my energy and then transformed into his advanced form. I looked over at Jurew and noticed his confusion, but after a second, he recognized me.

"Vollenth." he said.

"I believe Oyak thought that Jurrisk and I may have a better chance of getting through to the Third."

"Very well." he said.

After a moment, a light yellow aura surrounded Jurew and his eyes glowed a deep yellow.

"Jurrisk."

"Vollenth."

Both of us, in unison, walked over to the door and reached for our symbols. The barrier lit up and gave us resistance, but we got through and touched our symbols. The symbols glowed beneath our palms and lit up the entire hallway.

The third symbol began to glow brightly, and then all of them went dark. The door opened. Inside, the room was a black swirling vortex that resonated dark energy.

"Vollenth...the Third has broken the table." Jurrisk said.

"Yes, I know." I said walking over to the vortex.

I reached into the vortex and disconnected Oyak's mind from my own. I reached my mind towards the Third's and then connected to him.

His mind was cold and dark. As an Untamable, the Third's mind had very few limitations, so I was surprised to find his mind so confined. I could sense a flood of emotion coming from his core. Loss, fear, and loneliness. The emotions were so strong that any other mind would be driven insane if they were ever experienced.

I approached him. A barrier blocked my way, but I went through it and placed my hand on his scales. He looked at me, and I saw his eyes were wet.

"Zeon...my host wishes to speak with you. Can you calm your mind?" I asked.

"Leave." he said quietly.

"Zeon, my host knew your host, and I'm sure he would be willing to share those memories."

His mind grew in size and became stable. I reconnected with Oyak and he appeared beside me.

The Third's mind was dark and cold but vast in size. Vollenth stood beside me in my advanced dragon form, but once I arrived, Vollenth transformed into his dragon form. The third Untamable stood before me. Like Vollenth, he was a large dragon with four powerful legs. His scales were various shades of black and gray, and his eyes were gray where the white would usually be. The iris of his eye was black with a light gray slitted pupil.

Jurew and Jurrisk appeared beside me. Jurrisk seemed small compared to the other Untamable's.

"Why do all of you come?" the Third asked.

"I need your help...I need the help of all the Untamable's."

"I am useless without my true host." the Third said.

"Jurrisk, Jurew, Vollenth...I wish to speak to the Third alone."

"Oyak that may not be wise. His mind won't stay completely stable if all of us leave."

"That doesn't matter. I need to speak to him alone."

Jurrisk turned into a stream of energy that flowed into Jurew. After a second, I felt him disconnect. After another moment, Vollenth disconnected from my mind and then the Third's.

The Third's mind grew colder and began to shrink in size. I closed my eyes and, enveloping the Third's mind, I transported both of us into my mind.

"Warmth." he said slowly.

"Yes...I thought that my mind would be a better place to talk."

"Host...the memories with my host are all I want."

"I see...if I give them to you will you help me?"

"Once and then a favor."

I closed my eyes and thought back on my experiences with Nana. I touched the Third and they flowed into him.

Chapter 41 The Battle

"Elkaizer elk mel selk elk melous belaka Alexed!" I yelled.

A dark portal appeared in front of me. I closed my eyes and connected to the Untamable's, and their energy flowed through me. I felt it changing my form. Out of the portal walked Alexed and a short time after followed Telver. I gathered energy from Jurrisk and used it to teleport Telver deep underneath the city, to where Jurew was waiting.

"So a match between me and the Untamable's...very well then." Alexed said.

Alexed created an energy blade in his right hand.

"You sound confident." I said.

"Well, you have just handed me the Untamable's."

"I won't be that easy to defeat, Alexed."

"I was a contestant long before you, and over the years, I've learned many lessons, but the most important one is that the council is weak because they obey the ancient laws."

"Not all Councilors obey the ancient laws."

"Balka meleous elkai selk meleous elkaizel!" I yelled.

A river of energy shot up from the towers depths and flowed into me. I felt the trillions of minds connect with my own and all their energy flowed into me. Time seemed to slow as I thought back on the day's events.

"Oyak, thank you for my hosts memories." the Third said.

"Will you still help me?" I asked.

"Yes." the Third said.

"Thank you, Third."

"Zeon." the Third said.

"Zeon...ahh, I see. Thank you Zeon."

I took control of my body and absorbed Zeon into an artificial host that I had brought with me. I put on the necklace and turned to Jurew.

"Don't lose him." Jurew said.

"I don't plan to." I said.

Jurew handed me his necklace, and I placed it around my neck with the others and connected with Jurrisk. Vollenth connected with me, and I felt the Untamable's energy flow through me.

Their energy strengthened me as it flowed through my veins. My eyesight was sharpened until I could see even the most miniscule detail, my physical strength seemed to have no limit, and my mind was reinforced with the experiences of all the Untamable's. I took a small amount of energy from each of them and used it to fuel the creation of a new form.

This new form represented all of the Untamable's powers, spread equally throughout one body. The form was similar to my advanced form with a few exceptions. Instead of the scales being pure white, they were a light gray color, and my talons were coated with Jurrisk's poison.

I transformed back into my normal form and entered my mind. In front of me stood the three Untamable's in their full forms. I seemed like an ant compared to them. Emotions flowed through them. The emotions were of joy, excitement, and apprehension, which quickly faded, and then of pride.

I opened my eyes and found Palvore standing in the doorway.

"You really don't enjoy being a councilor do you?" Palvore asked.

"Palvore, let us explain." Jurew said.

Palvore held up his hand and yelled, "Enough! Both of you are expelled from the council!"

"Palvore, this is my fault. Don't blame Jurew." I said.

"Oyak, I sense Jurrisk within your mind. Jurew willingly gave him to you and that makes him guilty of the same crime as you."

Something inside of me broke. The amount of rage emanating from me couldn't of been only my own.

"No...you refuse to see Alexed as a threat and that gives us a purpose to do this."

"Well, your purpose is over. Go to your chambers and wait for me to erase your memories."

Confusion and pure rage filled my mind. These emotions were mine, but they were too strong to only be mine. Emotion and energy flowed into me from an unknown source and empowered me to do things I never thought possible.

"No...we won't." I said coldly.

"Fine. I'll erase your mind here."

Palvore started walking towards me. A wave of anger shot through me and that fueled my desire to keep my memories. An energy barrier appeared around Jurew and me. When Palvore tried to break the barrier, he was thrown back against the wall with such force that he left a crater in it.

"Oyak...what's happening to you?" Jurew asked.

Emotions of all variety overwhelmed me, and I fled into my mind. Thousands of thoughts flooded through my mind all at once. They made me flee deeper into my mind. The thoughts kept increasing in number and intensity until I reached my breaking point. Then all was silent. I enjoyed the sudden silence for a few minutes and then looked around. Around me stood thousands upon thousands of true forms.

"How—" I started.

"Oyak...what the Original Sixth wrote about, I think you just achieved it." Vollenth said.

I looked around and counted trillions of different types of true forms within my mind. Every form was different, different sizes and different forms. The Untamable's were easily known due to their size.

"Over four trillion are here." Vollenth said.

"Why...why are all of you here?" I asked.

"We felt your emotions, the want and need for power and survival, so we came. We're here to help you." all of them said as one voice.

"The need for my memories...I see that's what you sensed."

"Your desires connected all of us to you...your need to survive connected all of us to you." they said as one.

"I see. Thank you...all of you. I assume—"

Pain overwhelmed all of my senses and I fell to my knees. My vision was clouded by red and yellow spots. I tried to call out, but all I could do was crumple into a ball within my mind.

"All of you leave. Your presences are overwhelming and killing him!" I yelled to the forms around me.

After a second they started to leave my host's mind. The last one left just as Oyak's hair faded to a deep gray color.

The only ones who stayed were Jurrisk, Zeon, and I...the three Untamable's. I brushed against Oyak and flowed energy over him. I relieved him of his suffering by taking it into myself.

Chapter 42 The Thin Line

I felt Vollenth's touch, and soon after, my suffering was relieved. I still felt tired and sore, but the pain had been numbed to nonexistence.

"What...happened?" I asked.

"We'll discuss it later. Someone else wishes your presence." Vollenth said.

I faded from my mind and opened my eyes to see Jurew standing over me.

"Jurew." I said.

"Oyak...what happened?" he asked

"He connected with every true form that can still think on its own." Palvore said.

I looked up and saw Palvore standing close to the barrier.

"Even Palex." I said.

Palvore looked surprised and then slightly curious.

"So you have connected with him?"

"Yes...yes, I have, and I understand why you keep disconnected from him for such long periods of time."

"I thought you might. Your sentence will be reduced to two weeks of being confined to your chambers."

"I see."

"Release the barrier and give me the Third and you'll be free to go."

"What about Jurew?"

"He shares in your punishment."

"Unfortunately, this punishment will have to wait until tomorrow." I said.

"Oyak, you're walking a very thin line. Release this barrier and go to your chambers."

"Jurew, go deep within the tunnels. If Alexed has anyone with him, I'll send them to you."

"Oyak, are you sure?"

"Yes...this is our one chance to do this."

"Very well then."

Jurew teleported away, and I sensed him in the deep tunnels.

"This has gone far enough. Oyak, if you don't—"

I released the barrier and then created a stronger one around Palvore using some of the Untamable's energies as well as some of the leftover energy from the other true forms.

"Thank you...Original." I said before teleporting away.

The forms' energy strengthened my weakened form and every aspect of me along with it. I could feel the raw energy flowing through my veins, strengthening every cell throughout my body.

"Oyak, you won't be able to maintain this for long. We need to act fast." Vollenth said.

"I know, but I have to hold out until this is over."

I created an energy barrier around the towers roof using some of the Untamable's energy.

"Interesting...looks like if I kill you, I can gain more than just the Untamable's." Alexed said.

"That won't happen."

"That much power comes with a price. Your hair already grayed by at least another ten selections!" he yelled.

Alexed ran towards me. I dodged him and then threw him away with a wave of energy. I wasn't used to controlling this much energy so instead of throwing him a few feet, I ended up throwing him back a few dozen feet right into the side of the barrier.

"Oyak, let us take over. You aren't used to controlling this much energy." the Untamable's said.

"You aren't either...your energy is only a small lake within this ocean upon ocean of energy."

"We still have an advantage though. At least let us try." Vollenth said.

"Not yet...not until—"

Pain shot through my left leg. I looked down and saw that it was consumed in a deep purple flame. I felt Vollenth take control, along with Zeon and Jurrisk. The flames were extinguished within seconds, and then they returned control to me.

"Still so reliant on those Untamable's...so weak. That will never change." Alexed said.

"I may rely on the Untamable's, but with their help I can do anything."

"Not when bound by the ancient laws." Alexed said.

"Correct, but when I have the help of the others, I feel like I can ignore the laws."

"As a councilor, you can never ignore those laws." Alexed said mockingly.

"Your wrong...I can ignore them. I just have to accept the consequences that come with my decision."

"My organization has no laws, no limits." Alexed said.

"No, your organization has one law, unwavering loyalty to you and you alone."

"I wouldn't call that a law...a small request would describe it better."

I felt my concentration waver for a fraction of a second, and I knew that I didn't have long left.

"Let's finish this Alexed."

"I see you're starting to degrade...interesting."

Alexed created an energy blade out of purple energy. The blade turned dark purple while the rest of the sword remained a deep violet. I allowed the trillions of true forms to create a new form for me. The final result was a humanoid dragon form that utilized all of their unique abilities. My scales were a deep golden color and glowed brightly as their energy flowed through them. Nearly five hundred million forms flowed their essence and energy into a single scale on my new form. Just before every scale was strengthened, a burning pain wracked through my entire body. Before I knew what was going on, I had unleashed all of the energy that had built up within my scales. White light enveloped me, and I felt myself fading.

Chapter 43 The Being

Energy collapses on itself as it fades into nothingness, the user fades along with his foolish technique. The servant I revived so long ago looked at me with no recognition as he faded back, deep within the city. I sensed the second of the three returning to the tower and the one he fought returning to my servant's home. The First appeared as his current Sixth faded away.

"Bring him back. Now, Being!" the First yelled.

"That's against our agreement." I said.

"Killing him was against our agreement!" he yelled.

"He knew your position so that makes it a threat, that is against our agreement."

"He may know about me but not you. I've never mentioned you to him, and as long as that remains truthful then he is no threat to you."

"What will you give me in return?" I asked.

"Nothing because you killed him for no reason, you broke your own rules."

"No, I only bent, not broke."

"Revive him...please."

"Why this one...would you accept your first Sixth?" I asked.

The First hesitated for a moment and then said, "As much as I miss, him I'd rather have Oyak back."

"Hmm...you've changed Alakouse. Very well then."

I reached into myself and brought the Sixth back from the darkness. His energy was filling and would be missed, but the First was right in accusing me of breaking our deal.

I observed the revival process closely in hopes that I could recreate it in the future, but it happened instantly so I only observed a fraction of it. He faded away just as Oyak opened his eyes. Oyak looked exhausted.

"Oyak...it's good to have you back."

"Palvore...What happened?" he asked.

"I'll explain it in the future...rest now."

I could see him struggling to stay awake but eventually he succumbed and faded into his dreams.

I carried Oyak to his chambers and laid him onto his bed. Once I was out of his chambers, I began walking to my own chambers. Along the way, I decided to connect with Palex. My mind was a dark and cold place. Palex was mostly to blame, but considering all I've been through, I've also contributed to it on my own.

"Alakouse." Palex said.

"I need to connect to the others. Help me strengthen my mind for tonight."

"For what purpose?" he asked.

"I need their advice."

"The form's or Original's?"

"Original's."

"It won't be as easy as it was in the past. He's grown with Alexed's help."

"True, but I need their advice."

"Very well then. It will be ready by the time of your nightly meditation."

"No, prepare it for the dream world." I said.

"Sleep?" he asked.

"Yes."

"Very well. It will be ready."

Chapter 44 The Awakening

Grassy plains are all I can see around me. The sky is a deep blue color and there is a star shining in the distance.

"Beautiful...isn't it, Alakouse?" a voice asked from behind.

I turned and saw the Original second councilor staring into the sky.

"It's been a long time since I sought the council's advice." I said.

"The being has increased his defenses...this will be the last time you can seek our advice...although I think that I'm the only one who got through his barrier."

"This is our original construction isn't it?" I asked.

"I believe so. This was the first one that we presented to you. The Sixth and I created this before we presented it to you."

"Yes...I disapproved of almost every feature here."

"You've changed since then...I would of thought that you still care about us, but today's events prove otherwise."

"If everything goes along well, Oyak will be able to surpass all of the Originals...and hopefully he'll be able to kill him."

"You really believe that?" he asked.

"Yes."

"Well, let's hope your right".

"Oyak connected with all true forms that aren't absorbed."

"I know...we could sense it from inside."

"If I give him the gift, he will be able to hold them for longer...but it will attract the being's attention."

"This is what you need advice on?"

"Yes...what do you think is best for the council?"

"The best option for the council would be to avoid this...but I think for the situation with Alexed, you should give it to him."

"You never give a straight answer do you?" I asked.

"No, I like to keep things interesting."

"I see death hasn't lessened your sense of humor any."

"No, I don't think anything can do that."

"Since this may be the last time I see you, I need your advice on another subject."

"I only have a few minutes left, but go ahead."

"I'm going to retire soon."

"Alakouse...why?" he asked.

"Because it's time for me to rest."

"The council still needs you."

"My current Second councilor isn't ready for this...he'll never be ready."

"The Third?"

"No...not the Third, Fourth, Fifth, Eighth, Ninth, Tenth, Eleventh, Twelfth, or Thirteenth".

"Sixth or Seventh then."

"Oyak and Vollenth or Jurew and Jurrisk".

"Both Untamable's...interesting. Who has the most potential?"

"Oyak."

"Then choose Oyak."

"Jurew has potential, but it's locked away."

"Perhaps Jurew can become the new second councilor."

"Yes...but I fear that Velzeak will betray if he's not chosen."

"Do what you think is best for the entire council...if Velzeak will lead the council to destruction, don't choose him."

The Second began to fade.

"I'll have to leave now...you'll do what you think is best for the council."

Chapter 45 The Decision

"Due to recent events, I've decided to make this announcement. Starting tomorrow, we will begin preparations for an all out attack against Alexed and his organization. We will leave no survivors." Palvore said.

"Will we just ignore surrenders then?" Jurew asked.

"No. If they surrender, accept their surrender and teleport them to the tower's roof, but if they try to trick you in any way, then you are under orders to kill them."

"Why the tower's roof?" Jurew asked.

"I'll create a barrier around the roof before the battle begins that will hold them there until we can erase their minds." Palvore said.

"How much time before the attack begins?" Velzeak asked.

"Anywhere from today to late next week." I said.

"Oyak is correct. We don't have long." Palvore said.

"Is there anything else for this meeting?" Velzeak asked.

"Yes...yes there is. I've been thinking about this for quite some time, so don't say this decision is rushed. I believe that at least for the duration of this battle, two councilors deserve an advancement in rank." Palvore said.

"I don't think I agree, Palvore." Velzeak said.

"There are ways that I can overturn your description Velzeak, but I urge you to at least listen before making a choice."

"Go on."

"The current Sixth will change places with the Fifth, the Seventh will take the place of the current Sixth, and the Fifth will move to the Seventh's position. This will be in place only while we battle Alexed and the organization."

"No." Velzeak said.

"Reconsider, Velzeak. I would prefer not to have to overturn your choice."

"There is no one who can overturn my choice. The ancient laws state that for any action to happen, the top three councilors must agree."

"In the original meetings where Alakouse was the First councilor, he overturned his Second's decision twice using this method. You would know this if you read the transcripts like you're supposed to."

"The ancient laws have strengthened since the Originals days. Not all that Alakouse did is still right today."

"Fifth, Third, Thirteenth, do you agree with the decision?"

"Yes, I agree with it, but Velzeak is correct in saying that the top three are needed." the Third said.

"Fifth?" Palvore asked.

"I agree as long as it's temporary, but the Third is right." the Fifth said.

"It is temporary. It will only last through this fight. Thirteenth, what is your decision?" Palvore asked.

"Very well, Palvore. I agree." the Thirteenth said.

"Good. The council is made of thirteen and balanced by the top three. It can also be balanced by two in the upper council and two in the lower council. The decision made with either markup is valid under the ancient laws." Palvore said.

"The law states that the top three must agree!" Velzeak yelled.

"No, Velzeak. It states that the council's decision must be balanced as a whole. Usually it's the three most powerful Councilors, but at the moment, it's two in the upper council and two in the lower council, me and the Third, the Fifth and the Thirteenth. All of us in this new balance agree, and it overturns your decision, Velzeak." Palvore said.

"Is this meeting over, First?" Velzeak asked.

"Yes, I suppose it is...the current chamber arrangement won't change due to this being temporary, dis—."

"No, it's not over, not until all thirteen are dead!" A voice above yelled.

I looked up and saw a being in a dark cloak floating above the meeting table. After a second, a dark gray aura consumed him and then began expanding outward.

"Councilors, create a barrier around you infused with your form's energy. NOW!" Palvore yelled.

I created the barrier and then watched the entire room be consumed by the aura. I heard a loud cracking noise and then I passed out.

Chapter 46 The Preparations

"Oyak, wake up." a voice said.

"Oyak, I'll numb the pain soon, but you need to wake up now!" Vollenth said.

I opened my eyes and tried to get up. Pain washed over me, and I slumped back down. My vision was blurry, and I could barely see. Jurew's face came into focus above me after a while. My head was pounding as I tried to get up again. I made it to my feet, but I still leaned heavily against the wall. I looked down and saw that my cloak was soaked in my own blood. I looked around the room and saw the Councilors strew about the room, some laying in the floor, others were leaning against the wall.

Palvore walked over to me and placed his hand on my chest, and I felt my wounds close.

"Thank you, Palvore." I said.

"Heal with the Untamable's if you can. Wait for the rest to be up if you can't."

Palvore walked towards the rest of the council. I just stayed where I was and waited for my vision to return to normal. Once it had, I looked around the room and then saw him. The former Fifth was lying near the ruins of the meeting table in a pool of his own blood. The rest of the council began gathering around his corpse. Jurew and I joined them after I was confident I could walk.

"We'll have time to mourn later...we need to check on the citizens now." Palvore said.

"Yes...if we were attacked, then they were as well." I said.

"The top five councilors remain in the tower. The rest of you split up amongst the city and report any disturbances. Dismissed."

The lower rank councilors left and the top five remained in the ruins of the meeting room.

"As some of you know, when a councilor dies, we must perform a technique that releases their mind from their body and lets them rest in the air as pure energy. The question now is who should attend?"

"Traditionally the top three councilors attend and the rest are oblivious to the technique." Velzeak said.

"Yes, but I think the First has another idea." the Third said.

"Perceptive of you, Third...I believe that all of the remaining council should attend."

"That goes against tradition...although it seems you enjoy breaking tradition lately, so I suppose it's fine." Velzeak said bitterly.

"Velzeak, if you have something to say then say it." Palvore said.

"The decision to overturn my vote is an ignorant choice and is in direct violation with the ancient laws."

"The transcripts of the forty fifth meeting record states that Alakouse made a decision where his Second disagreed with him. He then received two votes in the upper council and two votes in the lower council and that overturned his Second's decision."

"It goes against the ancient laws!" Velzeak yelled.

"Velzeak, the decision is only temporarily...after Alexed is dealt with, everyone will return to their previous position."

"Not the former Fifth." the Fourth said quietly.

"We'll deal with it when it comes time." Palvore said.

"All except the Second are dismissed. The rest of you may rest or join the search. It's your choice."

All of us nodded and then left. I decided to join the search. The Third joined me, but the Fourth left for his chambers.

"Any idea why the Fourth isn't joining us?" I asked.

"The Fourth was very close to the Fifth...former Fifth. He helped him get into the council like you tried to do with Nana." the Third said.

"I see...I understand then."

"Let's go. I'll go to where the final three councilors are searching." the Third said.

"I'll join the search with the Sixth to Eighth."

"I'll see you when you get back, Fifth."

"I'll see you then." I said.

Fifteen citizens had been killed. Once we were finished searching, we erased the rest of the citizen's minds and returned to the tower.

Chapter 47 The Ritual

After all of us had rested for a few hours, we gathered in a room deep within the tower. All of us said a few praises about the Fifth. His body lay on a table made of a deep blue stone. Once everyone was finished, all of us placed our hands on the table and flowed energy into it. The table began glowing, and the Fifth's body transformed into pure energy, filling the room with a light blue glow.

As the glow faded, Palvore said, "All of you may leave...this ritual is over."

The Fourth and I stayed behind for a few extra minutes.

Turning to him I said, "I know what you're going through...it will get better with time, and as long as you remember him, he will never truly be gone."

"Thank you, Oyak."

I left the Fourth to his mourning and walked to the roof of the tower. Once I arrived, I noticed that Palvore was sitting on the edge of the tower.

"Oyak, I see I predicted correctly. I assume that you have questions."

"You saved me. Why couldn't you save him?" I asked.

"That is a complicated subject...unless you become the Second councilor, you won't ever truly get an answer." Palvore said.

"Why do you hide your identity?" I asked.

"That's a complicated subject as well."

"Is there any subject that isn't complicated?"

"For the rest of the council no, but for me, every subject is complicated."

"Why change your name if you'll just remain in the same position?"

"The person Vollenth remembers me as worked his way from Thirteenth to First councilor."

"You're still the same person...why hide it?"

"What do you remember before you were revived?"

"Nothing."

"A dark and cold place, barren of all emotions, lights in the distance are all that remain of everyone else in this realm." Palvore said.

"I don't understand."

"That is how the Original Second councilor describes the place where everyone goes after the body's death."

"The Original Second was killed?"

"Yes...everyone who retires is—" Palvore trailed off.

"Is what?"

"The next selection is coming up...once this battle is over, I'll finish that sentence." Palvore said.

"I'll hold you to that, Alakouse."

Chapter 48 Our Battles

As I was walking back to my chambers, I ran into the Fourth, and we passed each other without exchanging a word. Once I arrived at my chambers, I took off my cloak and fell into a deep slumber as soon as my head hit my bed. Instead of giving into my dreams, I connected with Vollenth and experienced his dreams with him. Our fantasies were interrupted when I heard a sound and jerked awake.

I scanned the room for the source of the noise, but when I found nothing, I got up and sent out a weak energy shock wave that engulfed the entire chamber. Near my chamber door stood a figure in the shadows. The shockwave had disrupted the technique they were using to hide.

"Who are you?" I asked.

The figure released the technique and stepped out of the shadows. At first I didn't recognize him, but after a second I saw it was Telver.

"Telver...you look different."

"You're not the same as last time either." he said.

Telver appeared to have aged several selections since the last time I had seen him. His hair had turned a deep silver color, his eyes were sunken in and showed no emotion or regret for what he had become.

"Let's finish this on the tower's roof." he said.

He opened a portal to the roof and walked through. I opened my own portal and followed him to the roof.

Once I arrived at the roof, I saw Telver had already created an energy blade and was in a fighting position on the far side of the roof. The cool night air felt cold against my skin as I walked to a position opposite of Telver. I created a simple energy blade using only my own energy and got into my fighting stance.

"This will be our last fight...let's make it worthwhile. Let the entire city tremble beneath us as our blades cross." Telver said.

"What happened to you?" I asked.

"You ruined everything...if Palvore hadn't pointed out Velzeak's change, then I would've accomplished everything...the First would of been Velzeak and I would of been Second, but instead you had to win and ruin everything. Now the only way to win against you is to destroy myself along with you." he said.

"Full true form combination...and energy manipulation, that's why your appearance has changed so much...your body couldn't handle it, but you went through with it anyway."

"Die." he said calmly.

Telver unleashed a wave of energy that covered the entire roof in a matter of seconds. I transformed into my advanced form and flew above it just before it reached me. He teleported above me and pushed me out of the air with another energy wave. I was forced to the roof, back into his original wave.

My scales protected me from most of the wave's effects, but the wave still engulfed me until it dissipated down the sides of the tower. Before I could move, Telver was behind me and cut deep into my back.

I pushed him away with an energy shock wave and created a barrier around myself. I reached behind me and felt the wound. It was deep and ran across my lower back. Hot blood was pouring out of the wound, and I allowed Vollenth to seal the wound and start to heal the internal wound. Vollenth sealed the wound in seconds, but the internal damage would take hours to heal if he was alone. The other Untamable's joined in, and it was fully healed after a few minutes.

I released the barrier and was about to attack Telver when both of us were distracted by a massive energy explosion near the upper left field. It consumed at least four citizen's homes. I sensed Jurew's energy weakening near the explosion.

"This will continue later." I said.

I ran to the tower's edge, jumped off, and spread my wings. I turned, heading towards where I saw the explosion. Telver unleashed his forms and followed me.

I turned and transformed into Vollenth's full form and grabbed Telver, throwing him to the bottom right field. I transformed back into my advanced form and continued to Jurew's location.

After a few minutes of flying, I landed on the edge of the crater. Jurew was nearby laying on the ground struggling to get up. Out of the ruins of one of the homes walked someone in a light brown councilor's cloak. He had a young complexion, but his eyes seemed to be much older and full of wisdom. They were pale blue in color, his hair was short, unstyled, and sandy blond in color.

I walked over to Jurew and helped him up while staring at the being near the ruins. I transformed back to my normal form and started slowly healing Jurew's wounds.

"Is that who I think it is, Jurew?" I asked.

"Ha...la...kouse." Jurew said slowly.

"The other Untamable...I assume you've killed Telver already?" Halakouse asked.

"No, I just threw him across the city so I could help Jurew." I said.

"Jurew doesn't deserve you help." Halakouse said.

"Why is that Halakouse?" I asked.

"He betrayed me. He cares for no one!" Halakouse yelled.

"How many have you killed Halakouse? How many citizens' lives have you taken?"

"None. Not all of his servants are required to kill, and I only agreed to kill one."

"Where are you in his servants...the top, the bottom, or somewhere in the middle?"

"If you would of just killed Telver, I would of been his top servant, but you're too weak."

"Oyak...help me make him understand." Jurew said.

"The offer to join still stands. Oyak, Alexed's organization is better than the council could ever be. We aren't limited by the ancient laws." Halakouse said.

"At what price?" I asked.

"The only price is that you allow me to kill Jurew."

"And if I refuse?" I asked.

"Then I'll kill both of you."

Halakouse launched a concentrated energy sphere at me and Jurew. I created an energy barrier around us using the Untamable's energy. The sphere exploded on impact and disintegrated the rubble of the homes around us. Once the smoke cleared, I saw he was preparing to launch another one, so I disconnected from Jurrisk and gave him back to Jurew so he could finish healing him.

"Don't...kill him, Oyak." Jurew said.

"I don't plan on killing him. I plan on giving him his true memories back." I said.

I teleported in front of Halakouse and grabbed his arm and yelled, "Jurew didn't betray you...he considered betraying the council to keep your mind intact!"

"Lies!" he yelled.

Halakouse created another sphere and tried throwing it at me, but I created a barrier around us and threw him to the other side. Halakouse slammed against the barrier, the attack faded away and before he could recover, I connected to his mind.

His mind had a warm and cozy feeling to it. Halakouse was nowhere to be found, but in his place were twenty unbroken true forms.

"You're not broken...your host hasn't broken you yet?" I asked.

"We agree with our host's ideals, so he has no reason to break us." they said as one.

"Why betray the council?"

"Each councilor that didn't choose us betrayed us. Our host was betrayed when his mind was destroyed by the councilors who betrayed us." they said.

"Once a contestant becomes a councilor, they don't get to choose a specific form, a form just comes to them. And your host...he was lied to, his mind manipulated to think that he was betrayed." I said.

"Lies!" they yelled.

"I'm not lying...search through my mind. See that I'm not lying."

"Your forms would destroy us."

I reached down and grabbed Vollenth's and Zeon's artificial hosts, took them off, and put them in my pocket. I severed the additional connections between us and then lowered my mind's barriers.

The twenty forms flooded my mind and began searching through my memories. I sensed another presence along with the twenty, but I decided to not interrupt their search. As they searched, I experienced all the memories they found, but once they got to my memories of Nana, I stopped watching and retreated deep within my mind. Once the twenty and the other had finished, they retreated back into their mind.

I returned to my body and opened my eyes. Halakouse was staring at me. I reached into my pocket, pulled out Vollenth's and Zeon's artificial hosts, and then placed them around my neck and connected with both of them.

"Oyak, you must warn us if you plan on doing that again!" they both roared.

"We can argue about it later...I have to finish this now." I said.

"Do you believe me now, Halakouse?" I asked.

"Yes." he said.

I released the barrier around us and transformed back into my advance dragon form.

"Good...are you willing to help the council?" I asked.

"Even if he is, it's too late...at least for Jurew and Jurrisk." Alexed said.

I turned and saw Alexed had stabbed Jurew through the heart and took Jurrisk's artificial host. Alexed pulled his blade from Jurew's chest and let Jurew fall.

"Halakouse, I'll give you one chance to make up for your betrayal. Kill Oyak and give me his true forms." Alexed said.

"No...you lied to us. I won't obey any of your orders!" Halakouse yelled.

"Then the only use you have left is to be someone whom I can torture and kill later!" Alexed yelled.

A dark gray barrier appeared around Halakouse and completely surrounded him. Alexed looked over at me and smiled.

"Only one of the three left. Time to finish this." Alexed said.

A massive burst of black energy exploded from the distance. A large fireball shot above the city and fell to the ground in front of me. The flames dissipated and out from them came Palvore in his black councilor's cloak. A thin strip of black flames ran down the sleeves of his cloak and his eyes glowed a bright gray color.

"Oyak, stay out of my way during this fight." he said.

"Ahh...the high and mighty Alakouse. Just in time to watch me complete my Untamable's collection." Alexed said.

"Two councilor's deaths have been caused by you now...I won't allow another." Palvore said.

"You won't be able to stop me...once I kill Oyak, I'll have full access to all the true forms!" Alexed yelled.

Alexed teleported in front of me and started slashing wildly at me. An energy sphere flew from behind me and knocked Alexed back a few feet. I looked back and saw that Halakouse had broken out of the barrier and transformed into a golden humanoid dragon form.

While Alexed was still distracted, I rushed at him and took Jurrisk's host. Then I teleported beside Halakouse. I placed Jurrisk's host around my neck then transformed into my golden dragon form.

"Kill him, kill him, kill him, kill him!" Jurrisk yelled within my mind.

A river of black flames consumed Alexed and pushed him a few rows away.

"Oyak, teleport that follower and Jurew's corpse to the top of the tower." Palvore said.

"Palvore, he may be of some use." I said.

"Follow my orders!" Palvore said.

"What if I personally vouch for him?" I asked.

"Oyak, I don't have time for this. Either teleport him to the tower or I'll kill him!" Palvore said.

"Very well, First." I said bitterly.

I teleported Jurew's body to the tower and then turned to Halakouse.

"Oyak, I think you'll have more use of these." he said.

Halakouse took off his artificial host and handed it to me.

"Thank you...farewell." I teleported Halakouse to the tower near Jurew and then turned to Palvore.

"I'm aware that Jurrisk wants revenge, but I think he would do better to help you in your fight."

"I can survive with only two Untamable's. Take Jurrisk and let him get his revenge."

"My form doesn't play well with others." he said.

"Then let me help you kill Alexed."

"This isn't your fight...you have your own enemy to deal with."

"Pal—"

Palvore teleported me away before I could finish. I looked around and saw that I was near the bottom right field. A metallic stench hit me once I started towards the field. Looking around, I saw dozens of corpses strewn along the edge of the field. At the center of the field sat Telver, atop a pile of corpses. His sword lay across his lap, and his eyes followed me as I moved in closer.

"I see you've finally finished your business with that traitor Halakouse. Now our battle should be uninterrupted until our end."

"This should of turned out differently...it's too late for that now." I said.

"Yes...although I believe we have different preferences to that statement." Telver said.

The shadows of ten broken true forms appeared around Telver. All of them flew to the edge of the field and turned to pure energy as they formed a barrier around the entire field.

"The Untamable's versus my own hundred and eighteen. Let's see who will win." Telver said.

"Let's finish this, Telver."

Telver picked up his sword and leapt into the air. As he descended, the entire field burst into flames, burning everything in sight. After a few minutes, the flames died down, and Telver and I stood at opposite ends of the burnt field.

The field had been completely destroyed along with everything on it. All of the corpses of the citizens who had been killed were gone, along with the lush green grass. I created an energy blade with the energy of the twenty true forms that Halakouse had given me.

Telver and I began slowly walking towards each other. Even though we didn't speak, we both knew what each other was thinking. The thought that ran through both of our minds was to finish this once and for all. Once we were within a few feet of each other, we stopped and stared at each other. Telver started resonating dark energy. After a few seconds, dark energy saturated his entire body.

"Two of the three Untamable's are dragons who have immense fire resistance. Let's see how far that resistance goes when I use all of the true forms' energy to burn you." Telver said.

Black flames ran along Telver's arm, similarly to that of Alakouse's true forms. The flames jumped from his arms and completely consumed me. After a few seconds, it became apparent that I needed to escape. The flames began to melt through weaker patches of scales and started to burn my flesh beneath.

I transformed into Zeon's full form and flew up into the air to escape. Zeon had a better resistance to black flames than Vollenth did. Once I was out of range of Telver's flames, I transformed back into my golden dragon form. Small patches of scales had been burnt away and left the flesh underneath exposed. Vollenth and Zeon started regenerating the scales while I stayed in the air. Telver didn't stay where he was for long. The flames on his arms dissipated as he rose to my level.

"Impressive Telver, but it won't work again." I said.

"I don't plan on using it at any rate, it would be too easy then." he said.

Telver and I returned to the field and retook our fighting stances and began slowly circling each other. Telver was the first to strike, lunging at me, wildly swinging his blade at me with no regard for his own defenses. I was able to land an overhand blow that left a gouge from the top of his right shoulder to the left side of his waist. Telver jumped back a few feet, and his forms healed the wound in seconds.

"Your form's energy won't last forever. If you plan on killing me, then you'll have to defend yourself along with attack." I said.

"I don't need any advice from a pathetic councilor!" he yelled.

Telver unleashed a wave of dark energy that consumed the entire field. I flew above the initial wave, but Telver unleashed half a dozen more until I was caught. I allowed Zeon to take over, and he transformed into his full form and consumed the entire wave, unleashing a condensed fireball at Telver. The fireball missed Telver directly, but once it hit the field, half the field was consumed by black flames.

I took control and transformed back into my golden dragon form and absorbed the leftover flames. Telver struggled to get up. Once he did, I saw that the flames had burnt through his forms and had destroyed his upper body. Telver stumbled forward, coughing up blood. Once he regained his footing, I saw his forms begin to reverse the damages done to him, and after a few seconds, he was completely healed.

"Telver...you know that the council can heal you. If we stop this, then I will use the Untamable's to heal you." I said.

"Even with the Untamable's, even with the remaining councilors help, you couldn't heal me, not fully. And even then you'd just erase my mind and kill me anyways."

"No. If you told us willing everything about Alexed's organization, then I promise you that you will be spared."

"And my memories?" he asked.

"I can't save them. In time though, after Alexed and the organization are destroyed, I may be able to get you back on the contestant list."

"So all of this can begin again? No, no Oyak. I won't surrender. Neither of us will survive through this day."

Telver pulled his artificial host from underneath his shirt and created a barrier around him. He gripped the host tightly, and then after a few seconds, the barrier exploded. I was thrown away when the barrier exploded. I was thrown into the barrier at the edge of the field. As I hit the barrier, I heard my wings bones snap, and the air was knocked out of my lungs.

Once I was able to breathe again, I began healing my wings and then looked up. Telver had changed. His hair had completely lost its color, but he looked several selections younger, and his eyes were a deep gray. I noticed that his artificial host had grown dormant, and his energy pool was growing by the second.

"Telver...very well then." I said.

"The councilor's life changed you, the Oyak I knew hated the thought of becoming what you are."

"You didn't deserve to become a councilor, not then...and not now." I said.

"What gave you the right to choose that?" Telver asked.

"Telver, what state would the council be if you had won, would you be first at this point?"

"Not at this time, but I would be Second and Velzeak, First."

"What state would the city be in? What state would it be in if the laws were abandoned?"

"Velzeak wouldn't of abandoned the laws. He would of strengthened them. He's not traitor. I already tried to convince him."

"When?"

"Before I entered your chambers, I visited him. He refused to join the organization even when I offered to betray Alexed and have him become the leader of it. He still refused to betray the council."

"So even you considered betraying Alexed? Could you defeat him?" I asked.

"I only considered it this last time. Do you know what he did to me when I failed to capture you?"

"Telver, the council could of helped you. You should of come to us when you were given your memories back."

"I had no desire to come running to the council. I would of just been killed!" he yelled.

"No...we would of helped you, and then your name would of been called in a selection soon after." I said.

"That would be against the laws. Once my memories were back, I killed most of our generation!"

"Certain members of the council would of convinced Palvore to spare you."

"No, Velzeak obeys the laws. He would of killed me himself."

"There would of been ways to keep you alive but also obey the laws. If you would of tried then, so many citizens would still be alive."

"Oh, 'so many citizens would still be alive.' you mean Nana would of been alive."

"No, not just Nana, All that you and Talakouse killed would be alive!" I yelled.

"You have to admit that the organization has some appeal, no restrictions, and most of all, no ancient laws."

"Some of the ancient laws are there for a reason. I don't agree with all of them, but I don't think the city would survive without them."

"You're wrong...I only wish that both of us could live to see the complete destruction of the council."

"I wish that you would of surrendered when we met at that home...I truly do. Let's finish this, Telver."

"Yes, lets!" he yelled.

Telver created an energy blade made out of his forms that equaled a tenth of Vollenth's energy pool. I created an energy blade combining all three Untamable's abilities and about a tenth of each of their energy pools. I relaxed into a fighting position that I studied in a scroll about the Originals in the towers library and was surprised when it felt natural to me. Telver took the fighting position that we had learned as contestants. I considered joining him, but I decided to stay where I was.

We stared at each other for several minutes, and then I lunged at Telver. He blocked my attack and threw me into a portal that he made. I was teleported high into the air. When I looked down, I only saw flames. Once I fell into the flames, I felt all my scales begin to melt away. I screamed as the flames burnt my flesh. I tried to absorb the flames, but once I failed, I connected with Halakouse's twenty and the rest of the forms and overwhelmed the flames with various flames from different forms until I completely extinguished the flames around me.

I slowly got up and allowed all the forms to instantly heal my wounds. Afterwards, I disconnected from all of them except the Untamable's and the twenty.

"I see you've learned to enhanced them." I said.

"Yes...now I won't use them, it'll ruin the fun."

I teleported my sword back to me and retook my previous position. Telver took a different fighting stance.

"So you still have some surprises, interesting." I said.

"You know very little about what I've become and everything that I've learned."

Telver ran at me. I slashed at his stomach, but he dodged it and then teleported behind me and slashed open my lower back. I turned and grabbed at his sword, losing my grip due to the amount of blood on it. I ended up being stabbed in the shoulder. Before he could pull his blade out, I wrapped him in my wings and unleashed a fireball that threw him across the field into his own barrier. The twenty began to heal my wounds while I caught my breath.

Telver and I continued to battle until the light faded from the city. Over the course of the battle, we covered the field in our blood and burnt it away several time over. We fatally wounded each other dozens of times, and just as light was beginning to appear over the city, we drained most of our forms' energy reserves.

We ended up on opposite sides of the field. One of my wings had been crippled and my right leg was almost completely useless. Telver had a bleeding gash on his right side. His artificial host glowed slightly, and I sensed him absorbing the remaining energy from it. Telver healed the gash and then collapsed to his knees, coughing up blood. I absorbed the remaining Untamable's energy. The twenty had ran out of energy long ago. I was able to heal my wing and leg, but the strain caused me to return to my normal form and cough up blood like Telver.

Telver and I stared at each other for a while, then both of us got up and began walking towards each other. I released the technique holding my sword together and absorbed the leftover energy. Telver did the same thing. Once both of us were at the center of the field, we stopped. I saw Telver concentrating all of his remaining energy into his right hand and preparing for a final technique. I flowed my remaining energy into my chest and took a deep breath. I released my breath as a final, condensed fireball. Telver unleashed his energy as an energy wave. As they collided, both of us thought, *I will win this.* The techniques threw both of us back. As I fell back, I saw the barrier around the field shatter. As it did, my mind went blank and I fell into unconsciousness.

Chapter 49 A Power Only He Can Possess

I lazily opened my eyes, my entire body aching. I could barely move. A sharp pain erupted from my chest, sapping all of my strength as I tried to move.

"So...close...so close." Telver said slowly.

I looked over to where Telver was and saw that he was still. I struggled to my knees and found a dagger plunged into my chest, only a few inches from my heart. Without thinking, I pulled the dagger out of my chest, and pain shot through my body. I fell back to the ground as blood poured out of the wound and pooled around me.

I slowly crawled over to Telver and took his artificial host, placing it around my neck. I accessed his forms and used them to close the wound and heal the rest of my wounds. Once I was able to stand, I started using what little energy I had recovered to heal the broken forms within the host.

"Oyak, bring Telver's corpse up to the tower's roof. Don't delay." Palvore said.

"We should go Oyak." Vollenth said.

"I'll go once I'm finished healing the broken forms." I said.

I looked out into the city. The light had almost covered it, then I saw the dozens of corpses scattered around the streets and even more wounded citizens lining them.

"The battle took many." Vollenth said.

"Alexed is still alive...Palvore doesn't have the strength to kill him. Once we recover, we'll have to finish it." I said.

"Oyak...will you destroy me?" Jurrisk asked.

"Why would I?" I asked.

"Without my true host alive, I don't want to live."

"Your true host will be brought back...one way or another, Jurew will live again." I said.

"Oyak, the broken are healed. We need to get to the tower." Vollenth said.

"Yes...yes, we do."

I closed my eyes and opened a portal to the tower's roof and carried Telver's corpse through it. Waiting for me on the roof was Palvore and a few other council members.

I dropped Telver's corpse on the roof and walked over to Halakouse and said, "Your true forms helped me in the fight. Thank you."

Halakouse remained silent.

I looked around and saw everyone staring at me.

"Halakouse was originally part of the organization, but he changed sides and helped me win my battle against Alexed's top servant."

"He was still a servant. He probably killed thousands." one of the councilors said.

"Alexed lied to Halakouse. He convinced him that Jurew had betrayed him. When he agreed to join the organization, he made it clear that he only wanted to kill Jurew, but by the time he turned to our side, he had kept that promise to himself and had refused to kill anyone else. When he did turn to our side, Alexed killed Jurew. Halakouse's hands are clean. He didn't even break the true forms he was given."

"I assume that he told you all of them. If so, you shouldn't trust a traitor's word." Palvore said.

"Actually the twenty forms he gave to me shared their memories with me."

"He could of altered their memories." another councilor said.

"I would of sensed anything altered. I didn't."

"Broken forms can be easily manipulated. They may believe that he didn't alter them but he actually did." another councilor said.

"His forms weren't broken!" I yelled.

"Enough! Oyak, we should talk alone. Councilors, take the traitor and leave."

I created a barrier around Halakouse and yelled, "Leave him!"

Palvore nodded, and they took away Telver's corpse and left us.

"Oyak, I don't feel comfortable talking about councilor secrets while a traitor is around."

"He turned, he betrayed Alexed, and you still call him a traitor?"

"He accepted Alexed's offer. I can't allow him to live."

"Palvore, you will not kill him. Alexed killed Jurew not him."

"Everyone who joined Alexed, even if they returned to our side, will die."

"No. I won't allow it."

"You won't allow it? You're not the First councilor. You have no authority over me."

"I have access to all of the true forms, and even with you being an Original, I can still defeat you with their help."

"Is that a threat, Oyak?"

"Yes, Alakouse. It is. I want you to bring back Jurew like you did with me."

"No."

"Bring him back."

"No, Oyak. I can't."

"Alakouse...please."

"I'm sorry, Oyak. I can't."

I connected with all of the true forms and yelled, "Bring him back Palvore. Now!"

"That won't change anything, Oyak."

"I'll kill you if you don't bring him back."

"If you attack me, I'll defend myself."

I concentrated all of the forms energy into my left hand and was about to charge Alakouse until I noticed a light emanating from Jurew's chest. The light glowed faintly. I stopped flowing the energy into my hand and walked over to Jurew. I looked closer at the light and sensed Jurew's energy and life force emanating from it. I placed my left hand onto his chest and concentrated on enhancing his life force and then I sensed Jurew somewhere. I concentrated on bringing him from that place back into his body.

Oyak walked over to Jurew, all the while staring at his chest. Once he reached him, he kneeled down, placing his dominant hand on Jurew's chest. He flowed all of the true form's energy into his chest.

"Alakouse, he's reviving him." Palex said.

I looked closer at them, and soon I saw Jurew begin to breath. I started to sense his life energy flowing through him again. I felt Oyak's life force begin to fade, and I noticed his hair began to lose color. Once his hair had completely lost all of its color, his connection with the true forms vanished, and he collapsed next to a fully healed Jurew. I walked over to them and stared at Oyak.

You were able to accomplish something I never truly will...you will receive the position once it comes to it.

I closed my eyes and teleported Oyak and Jurew to their respective quarters.

"This complicates matters with him." Palex said.

"Yes it does. I'll deal with it before he kills both of them."

"Don't give up what you truly need to keep."

"I'll try not to...it may be the only solution though."

"I'd rather disintegrate into nothingness than be with his collection."

"If it happens, go to my successor and empower him."

"Very well, old friend."

Chapter 50 The Revival

I rolled over onto my back and opened my eyes. I was looking at my chamber's ceiling through blurred eyes. Blinking a few times to clear my vision, I slowly sat up and looked around my chambers.

"Oyak, I'm sorry to interrupt your thoughts, but I need to speak to you in my chambers." Palvore said within my mind.

"I'll be there soon." I said.

I used my bedside table for support as I stood, my entire body aching.

"Oyak, take it easy. Me and the others are still healing you." Vollenth said.

"How long have I been asleep?"

"Five or six hours." Zeon said.

"What happened? I remember seeing something in Jurew's chest and then it's all black."

"You revived him with the help of the rest of the true forms...thank you, Oyak." Jurrisk said.

"So Jurew is alive...good."

I changed into a fresh cloak and then started for Palvore's chambers.

When I arrived at Palvore's chambers, I found his door open. I walked to the entrance and was greeted by Palvore.

"Come in Oyak. Shut the door behind you."

I walked in and shut the door behind me.

"What is it you wanted to discuss Palvore?"

"I asked you here to discuss Alakouse with you."

"You asked me here to talk about your past self?"

Palvore walked over to his bed and picked up a book wrapped in faded cloth. He looked at it for a while and then unwrapped it. The book was bound in a thick black material, there were ornate runes covering the front. At the center of the cover was a gemstone that was scarlet red on one side and a deep vibrant blue on the other. Palvore walked over to me and handed the book to me. I looked at it for a few minutes and then tried to hand it back.

"No, you keep it for now. You'll need to study it if you're to succeed at replacing me."

"Replace you?"

"Yes, Oyak...this coming up selection I will retire, and you will replace me as the first councilor."

"What about Velzeak...he won't accept this decision."

"I will deal with him if he returns."

"He not here?"

"No, he's been missing since the fight."

"Is he alive?"

"Yes...but I can't sense where he is."

"Is he avoiding the council?"

"Yes...he's done it in the past."

"This isn't the time to abandon us."

"Oyak, Velzeak is many things, but he is not a traitor...we just need to give him time."

"How much time will you give him?"

"As much time as he needs."

"What if Alexed attacks and he's not there? He won't be fulfilling his duties as a councilor."

"Oyak, when Alexed attacks he'll be there...he won't betray the council."

"How can you be so sure?"

"Oyak...I've known Velzeak for a long time, and I know he won't betray."

I held up the book and said, "When he finds out about this, I wouldn't think of him so highly."

"He'll come through for us."

"So is this Palvore's journal or—"

"That journal is my journal from the Originals days."

"Alakouse's then."

"Yes...the first few dozen pages are just accounts of the first few meeting. After that is most of the information you'll need to review before becoming the first councilor."

"You act like the first few meetings were nothing."

"The first few meetings are nothing compared to the rest of the journal."

"Where does it end?"

"I stopped writing a physical journal after I stopped being known as Alakouse."

"I see...was there anything else?" I asked.

"Perhaps...yes, do you remember the sentence I said I'd finish after the battle?"

"I believe so...it was about what happens to the Councilors who retire."

"Yes...all those who retire are devoured."

"Devoured?"

"Yes, their bodies and minds are converted to energy which the ancient being devours."

"The ancient being?"

"The one who killed you and so many others over the years...also the one who revived you. I suppose you should sit. It will be a long tale."

Chapter 51 The Truth

"To fully explain this, I'll have to reveal some secrets that you can never reveal to anyone...if you do I'll have to erase you from everyone's minds permanently."

"I understand." I said.

"Good...good. There was a time before the ancient laws, a time of peace where we freely shared our powers with all of the citizens. The first few meetings were spent deciding if we should share all of our powers and abilities with each citizen. Eventually it was decided that we would share only the bare minimum with each citizen. That, along with a few other restrictions, was all grouped together and made into the first collection of laws made by the Originals."

"So the ancient laws weren't in effect yet?" I asked.

"No, they weren't in effect until everything fell apart...let's not jump ahead though."

"Sorry."

"Let's continue. There were no selections back then so it's hard to compare time from then to now, but I believe it was about twenty or thirty selections worth of time before anything significant happened. We began to notice some citizens were able to access and gather more energy than the rest of the citizens. After a few meetings, we decided to offer those beings, along with anyone else who thought they were up to the challenge, a chance to serve under us. We called those beings councilor servants. At first, a servant could only serve under one councilor and couldn't change councilors once selected."

"Were they tested like the contestants?" I asked.

"Yes...although it was harder to win, and unlike the selections, anyone could volunteer to try. Also, the selection could end with no winners. About two or ten selections worth of time passed before we allowed some of the servants to train under multiple Councilors and serve them. The servants mainly ran minor errands for the council and investigated any suspicious areas that were too minor for us to deal with. They were allowed to have a larger energy pool and learn more advanced techniques than most citizens."

"That sounds useful, why aren't they around now?"

"Their disbandment was part of the deal I was forced to make."

"What deal?"

"The deal that I made with the ancient being that allows him to devour all retired Councilors and everyone else who dies."

"Why would the first councilor make a deal that doomed the entire city?"

"I had no choice Oyak...he would of killed everyone if I had not made the deal."

"You couldn't of fought him?"

"Even with all of the true forms and all of the citizens powers, I couldn't defeat him, so what other choice did I have?" Palvore yelled.

"You should've given the citizens a chance. We would of fought alongside you and your servants until the being was dead."

"Oyak, you don't understand. The ancient being was unbeatable. He comes from the race who created us. We couldn't compete with his power."

"Couldn't you of isolated him somewhere and trapped him there until we grew stronger?"

"No Oyak. His power was—"

The entire tower started to shake, and both of us were knocked out of our chairs. After the shaking stopped, Palvore and I pushed the scrolls and books off of us and ran out to the balcony.

Outside we could see citizens running away from the rubble of their former homes, and Alexed's servants roaming through the city killing everyone they could find. Alexed was standing in the courtyard in front of the tower picking off any citizens who came close to the edge.

"Oyak, we'll continue this later. Go wake up Jurew, give him his form, and guide as many citizens into the tunnels as you can. Stay there and wait until Alexed is dead."

"Palvore."

"Yes wha—."

I used the Untamable's energy to knock him out and teleported his journal into my chambers. I then teleported Jurrisk around Jurew's neck. I connected with all the true forms and then teleported in front of Alexed.

Chapter 52 The Release

"Oyak...I was expecting Alakouse, but I suppose you'll be a good warm up."

"Alakouse won't be joining us. I'm the only one you'll be fighting today."

"Oh and why is Alakouse unavailable?"

"Currently he's knocked out in his chambers. It will be awhile before he recovers from the attack I used on him."

"I see...well, I suppose once I'm done with you, I'll have enough true forms to destroy the entire city."

"You won't win against me."

"We'll see about that."

I created a portal in front of us and said, "Let's go Alexed."

"I think the courtyard is more fitting for this fight."

I closed the portal and released Zeon into the physical realm and had him grab Alexed and fly him to the top left field. I reopened the portal and stepped out onto the field. Zeon joined me after a few minutes. He threw Alexed to the top of the field and then landed near me in the bottom of the field. I borrowed some of Palex's energy and created an energy barrier around the field.

"So this is where you want to die then. Fine. Die!" Alexed yelled.

I concentrated on all of the true forms that I was connected with and released all of them onto the field in their physical forms. The air became saturated with energy, the true forms all unleashing their full potential and their most powerful attacks.

Alexed was tossed between the forms for what seemed like hours, each true form just tossing him to the next. I just stood there and watched as Alexed was passed between the forms. When Alexed reached the left corner of the field, he unleashed a massive wave of dark energy that captured every true form in its path. Before it spread too far, I transformed the forms back into their normal forms and absorbed all of them back into myself.

The wave had captured only a dozen forms, but even such a small amount nearly doubled Alexed's energy pool. I transformed into Vollenth's full form and charged Alexed. Just as I neared him, I transformed into Zeon's humanoid dragon form. Alexed tried to stop my approach with more dark energy attacks, but Zeon's form protected me from most of them. Once I was within a few feet, I battled for control of his mind, and after a few seconds, I was able to take control.

Alexed's mind was dark and pitch black. I could sense locked memories that were from the Original's era but I ignored them. I grabbed at the collection of broken true forms and succeeded at absorbing a few thousand of them along with the dozen that he had just stolen. Once I captured as many as I could, I returned to my own mind and body and teleported to the other side of the field and began healing the forms' minds. Alexed was about to charge, so I healed all the forms' minds at once.

The strain from healing all of them got to me immediately, making me fall to my knees. I tried to regain the ability to think or even move. The thoughts of trillions of minds became too much for my mind to comprehend, so I disconnected from all of them except Vollenth, Zeon, and the few thousand that I had just healed.

I regained the ability to move, but by the time I looked up, Alexed was already on me. I tried to dodge his attack, but my movements were still sluggish. He was able to slide his blade deep into my chest.

"You lose, Oyak, and now I gain all of your forms."

"I lose...but you don't get anything."

I disconnected from all my true forms and transferred all of them to Jurew.

"Farewell Vollenth...help them kill Alexed for me."

Chapter 53 The Ancient's Names

"Councilor awaken. You're safe for now here within the mind of many." A voice said.

I opened my eyes and blinked away the blurred vision. I got up and looked around. I was laying in a grassy field that seemed to go on forever in every direction. There were various figures moving in the distance. Near me was someone dressed in a councilor's cloak, but I didn't recognize him. I got up and felt my chest for any trace of the wound Alexed had made.

"Who are you...where are we?" I asked.

"Most don't remember their first arrival, although yours was short, so I'm not surprised you don't know where this is."

"I would remember if I had been here before."

"Death has a striking ability to erase or suppress the unprotected minds. Even with all of your past training, you still have so much locked away potential."

"I thought when you died you were absorbed into the ancient being. I doubt he'd let people communicate like this."

"This is no trick Oyak. Over the...selections we have devised ways to communicate with the outside as well as with each other."

"You wear a councilors robe...what generation are you?" I asked.

"The Original generation. I am the second councilor. My name is Velvexs."

"You're the Original Second Councilor?" I asked in disbelief.

"Yes, I am...although when we first sensed you, we didn't expect you to be as well off as you are as a councilor now."

"What...did you expect then?"

"We expected you to give up after the first year. Most of the servants were not councilor material, at least not of the first generation."

"Servant...you mean I was a councilor's servant?"

"Yes...you were the first servant to receive training from anyone but your original supporter."

"Who was my supporter?"

"Alakouse."

"Why didn't he mention it?"

"How far into the story did he get to? Was he at the part where he made the ancient laws with the deal?"

"Partially. He only mentioned that the deal involved everyone getting devoured when they died."

"I see...when he made the deal, he involuntarily gave up a small part of himself. That part contains some of his memories, including the identities of his servants and the fine details of the deal."

"Fine details?"

"Yes...in Alakouse's current memories, the rest of the Originals were gradually retired over the first twelve selections. In reality, all of us were eliminated at once and replacements were chosen at random from the citizens."

"So the first twelve selections didn't happen?"

"Well, the first twelve that the citizens remember are actually the second twelve. The same goes for the Councilors."

"The...part of Alakouse that is here...is he stronger than the main Alakouse?"

"He contains a large amount of his main power however, the main Alakouse is still stronger. Well, we've rambled for quite some time now...I suppose it's time I tell you why we're talking to you."

"So there's a purpose to all of this?"

"Yes, time flows differently within the being. You have already spent over an hour in here, although in reality only a few seconds have passed."

"Why would there be a time difference?"

"The being consumes our energies and slowly feeds off them. He then reinforces them with his own energy. That energy speeds the decay rate of our mind's energy so to deal with that, he slows time within himself."

"How long would our minds survive if there was no time difference?"

"Only a few hours, maybe a day."

"We're rambling again." I said.

"Right, the entire original council decided to give you a chance to fully unlock your potential and receive guidance from all of us before you return."

"I'll be brought back again?"

"Yes, but it won't be for another few days outside of here, maybe a few weeks. It still doesn't give us much time. As Second Councilor, I was the one who taught you the basic versions of most of the forbidden techniques. I'll give you that knowledge again now."

Velvexs placed his hand on my forehead and flowed energy into my mind. Nothing happened at first, but then the memories began to flood my mind.

Chapter 54 The Differences

The flood of memories and the differences between my two lives made me stop and ask, "Who am I?" Eventually after some thinking, I realized that I know exactly who I am and who I was. **I am** Oyak the councilor, but **I was** Oyak the councilor's servant. Between my two lives, my opinions had changed greatly. In my servant days, I had less empathy, and I was, in general, more cold. Now I have a strong sense of empathy, but I still have enough coldness to be able to control my feelings and do my job as a councilor.

My old memories gave me a new perception of the world around me. These fields were a trick, they were just a memory projected into my mind along with the rest of the Originals. I looked at Velvexs as I did in the past and pondered what it would be like doing what he does now. I realized that I could relate to him the most, especially due to my new perception.

"I see you've remembered."

"Yes...the training, Alakouse's training, your training, all of it, everything about my past that I had forgotten I remember thanks to you."

"In order for you to save us, we need to be remembered in the mind."

"I had forgotten the speech was different. I need to kill Alexed and then start."

"I see you've adjusted back. There are other things I must teach."

"This isn't the original one is it?"

"Observant. No, during these long years we've changed from original."

"I see...time passes quicker than most." I said.

"He processes remnants of many forms still." Velvexs said.

"I would think devouring would have been mastered long ago. This is an easy weakness." I said.

"Once absorbed, it does so instantly."

"Still, I only had remnants of Untamable's."

"The rest were still remnants due to them giving you small portions. Only citizens would weaken."

"How many?" I asked cautiously.

"How many? How many? Are you really so ignorant of a citizen's life as to lead them to the slaughter just to weaken them and to strengthen and allow the Within to gain more advantage?" Velvexs yelled.

"I only wished to know so I could absorb energy enough to equal enough." I said defensively.

"If you betray, I'll make you suffer."

"None exist." I said coldly.

"I see...then we shall continue." he said.

"I'm prepared."

Velvexs connected with my mind and after a brief moment, our minds fused into one. Once our minds were fused we soaked in each other's knowledge and experiences and learned everything we could about each other. I felt years and eventually decades pass as we taught each other our well kept secrets. Once both of our memories had finished melding, our minds untangled from each other and we became two beings again.

"Interesting." I said.

"Learning the Original's lives has advantages." Velvexs said.

"Complex as it is, there are the advantages of truth and clarity."

"You've mastered it after only one attempt. It's interesting as in the past you had less chance."

"I observed Alakouse many times." I said.

"I suspected."

"I know."

"The rest wait." Velvexs said.

"We will meet before the departure, or have plans changed?" I asked.

"No."

"I'll see you then." I said.

"Alakouse is not Palvore." Velvexs warned.

"Yes."

"To meet soon." he said.

I nodded and turned. As I walked away time seemed to speed up that point. I met with the rest of the Originals and learned their secrets. I quickly learned that everyone had held back from my original training. Only a small drop in their oceans of knowledge was given to me then. Now I had full reign. Alakouse taught me the seldom used secrets of the city left to me, as well as Palex's secrets. The Seventh taught me how to harness dark impulses more than I already could and how to harvest the dead's energy and to preserve them such as the Within did to us. The rest of the Originals training was normal and unimportant in the long run. Once I had finished the last meeting and I was about to head back to meet with the rest once more, I felt a strange new presence in my mind.

"Who are you?" I asked cautiously.

"Silence from before creation, secrets from other gray to nought revel to lead to weakness for us." a cool voice echoed in my mind.

"I don't sense you within. Are you living?" I asked.

"No, only separate from yours and the devoured. I will show you if you will."

A portal ripped open the fields and led to complete darkness. I sensed an ancient and dark presence on the other side.

"Come, much left." he said slowly.

"What are you?"

"I am one of the Within's kind. Much left and answers follow once asked."

After a moment, I stepped through the portal and arrived at a much different place than what I had seen reflected.

Chapter 55 The Other

Dark swirling wisps of energy flooded my view as the portal closed behind me. I stared at the place in which I had arrived. Darkness was a major part of it, but small pockets of light suggested that the darkness wasn't all. I looked around and found no one around, but then I looked through the same places I had just scanned, relying on my senses rather than my vision, and I found him. He stood near one of the patches of light, tall and lean in form. His deep gray eyes opened and stared back at me. His skin was pale from lack of light, his hair was a light brown that was a sharp contrast to his gray eyes.

"Nice to meet One Who Should Not Be. After all the time the Within has spent trying to find you, I'm surprised he hadn't considered your true identity."

"What do you mean by, 'One Who Should Not Be'?" I asked.

"I come from a race with powers to create life, and you are one of those creations, just as everyone else naturally here is."

"You still haven't answered me."

"You were created with the energy worth more than a single being's worth and so you should not be."

"So I'm not welcome by your race?"

"My race will destroy you once they sense you."

"So you've come to speed the job up?"

"No. I was killed and captured shortly after the betrayal of the Within to my people."

"What do you want then?"

"You're not as such they taught as a one that should not be would behave anywhere else, and because of that, I believe that you should live and not be killed."

"Will your opinion hold?"

"It will never be heard from me, it will be heard once you kill the Within. I have carved the technique into the folds of the Within's powers."

"Will it prevent your rescue?"

"Mine yes, but the rest, no."

"Release it then. When I receive everyone, I need to not lose."

"I have worked since capture."

"I will not leave without your help."

"You will have it, but once you see an opportunity, you shall take it. I will give the rest time to flee to you and another."

"Another?"

"Do not take a burden upon yourself alone or your mind will rip itself."

"There is only me."

"Nana or Jurew will take burdens without need."

"You know the Untamable's?"

"Yes."

"What is this really about?"

"Before the fight comes to me, use the technique to open a portal and remember these patches of light. They are defects of the Within's within."

"Weaknesses then."

"Yes and no. Come to me once you are ready to win and then centuries of explanations will happen in seconds."

"Could I use the patches for an advantage?"

"No, they are too small of a gap to gain."

"You know more weaknesses?"

"Yes, I know many."

"You won't tell me now will you?" I asked.

"No, you must come to me when you decide to truly battle the Within."

"Very well then. It will be some time once I succeeded."

"Yes, you will take your time."

"Alexed is...connected with the Within and I need a way to sever them."

"Alexed is not truly connected, although one you will find shall be. The only minor connection he has is with the forms of the dead that he had given, as well as the deal he has made."

"What deal?"

"Once revived, he was given a choice, to die over again at that moment or to live and become the enemy of the council and destroy the city."

"So he gained life but at the price of the fragmented mind." I said quietly.

"No, the fragmentation was self made. He did it to survive the guilt of becoming what the council fears the most."

"A traitor." I said.

"I will teach you how to hide yourself from the Within as well as to seal all forms that have been made through a non physical state."

"I'll only have the Untamable's then."

"Palex will no doubt join you when he learns that he isn't the only one who knows about the other Alexed."

"How does Palex know I thought that all the forms' minds were erased after the deal was made?"

"They were, but Palex is no normal form. He needs to exist. He cannot be destroyed nor altered."

"I know he's special but not to this degree."

"Palex was created for Alakouse, although an almost opposite force is the Untamable white dragon Vollenth."

"Vollenth is powerful, but even I know he can't compare to Palex."

"Vollenth lacks proper power and energy, but he rivals Palex in knowledge and with you, experience."

"Alakouse has much more experience than I do."

"Yes, but you have the understanding of his experience. Now all of the rest of the Originals experience and knowledge rest with you as it should, One Who Should Not Be."

"I understand that title to be insulting, not of gratitude."

"If you interpret as such then fine, but if not, then embrace it as you make through the stream of time. I will give you two techniques. One to use once revived and one to give and remind Alakouse of its creation and to change the stream of the other."

"Stream of the other, what are you—"

The being grabbed me by my throat, held me up, and threw me into one of the pieces of light. Floods of memories raced through my mind. I saw the creation and destruction of many cities such as ours, their development and evolution over billions upon billions of years. Then I saw our city but different, as it was originally, but it existed elsewhere. It was out of this timeline.

"You have seen what most deem not. True it is and the technique called zero is the key to accessing and altering the timelines. The other will temporarily destroy the connection between connections of non physical content and connection between the forms and beings."

"The first is not needed. I'll get it once I decide to fight the being."

"No, it is necessary. He will retire and then use it before the battle will take."

"The next selection won't happen while the council is at war with Alexed."

"No, not the current battle. The battle after and after again with the Within."

"Teach me then. I don't have long left remaining."

"Zero cannot be mastered without performing it. I will teach you as best, the other will be given directly."

"I do not have time to make lessons." I said.

"Zero will not be begun. Hold out your dominant hand."

I held my left hand out in front of me with my palm facing upwards. The being touched the center of my palm and I felt a searing pain run from my palm up through my left arm. I jumped back in surprise and looked at my arm. From the center of my palm to my shoulder, I saw a black vein of energy flowing through my flesh.

"What is this?" I asked regarding to the vein of energy.

"That is the erasing technique."

"The technique is performed through a seal?"

"Yes. It utilizes the seal along with the desire to disconnect all non physical forms from the users within the city."

"Why didn't you mention the seal before?"

"I knew you wouldn't of acquired it if I told you that part."

"You shouldn't force a technique on a councilor like you just did."

"And why should I care about the policies and regulations of a councilor when I was on the council where you were created?"

"So if your kind has no respect for what you create, why even create us at all?" I asked failing to hold back my rage.

"Our kind creates what we will so we can watch it grow in some, but others want to watch them wither and die and absorb their suffering all the while enjoying their existences as long as the pitiful creations last."

"And no doubt you're the latter. All you want to do is watch as we suffer, so I'm glad you were captured within so when I kill it you will die along with it!" I yelled, fully releasing my rage.

"You have no idea what being held and fed off of for as long as I have feels like. I was once the former but through all the suffering and pain I've felt, I just want it to end."

"So that's why you won't leave."

"The reason I gave before is the true reason, this is only a secondary."

"The zero. Give it to me." I said bitterly.

"You must promise me that you will truly stay true to Alakouse's promise once he presents it, otherwise I will not allow."

"What is the promise?"

"To never use the technique."

"Why would he ask of that?"

"To preserve your life and not to shorten."

"The technique shortens the life?"

"No, but the Within does."

"I don't understand?"

"You will once presented and you will heal after your decision."

"Yes then"

"Good...good. The lines of time will confuse. I will give you a partial understanding once you leave."

"When I leave?"

"The complexity of this will not be known. You will wake up in life with the basic understanding of the lines of time as well as zero in your possession. The vein will fade as to hide my help from the Within."

"Very well then."

"Now that I'm thinking of it, I want to tell you that I will try my best to protect the Originals from the Within's wrath."

"Thank you."

"The rest are waiting...go to them, to the Originals."

The portal that brought me to the being reopened and I stepped through.

Waiting for me were the thirteen original Councilors. Alakouse stood in the front while the rest stood behind him.

"Welcome back. I assume the other Within informed you of the limited time."

"Briefly."

"The other...I is about to meet with the main within."

"Does he know about what has transferred?" I asked.

"No." Alakouse said.

"Does he know about the other within?"

"No." Alakouse said.

"Very well then. Let's continue."

"Yes, let's." the Seventh said.

"What shall I do?" I asked.

All except the second councilor disappeared and the land began to flicker in and out and in their place was endless darkness.

"The others have left to begin the conversation with the Within. I must join them soon and to do—"

"Release me back into the darkness, I'm ready." I said quickly.

"You aren't, but I don't have a choice anymore...farewell Oyak, a councilor and a councilor's servant to the Originals."

The fields disappeared completely and I returned to my own mind and was bound there. I tried to move but I couldn't. My mind began racing, and I began to panic, but then I remembered where I was and stopped. Once I relaxed, I was able to think about what I had learned in the past years. While outside, only a few weeks had passed. To me, it was almost an entire century that had passed. I was content with what had happened, and I let my mind wander into my memories of both of my pasts.

Chapter 56 The Technique

Suddenly the flow of memories were interrupted and then they stopped. I felt something cold beneath me and realized that the Within had revived me. I took a shaky breath and open my eyes. All around me was darkness, but above me, I could make out the worn textures of an ancient mural. The mural had not held up to time and was mostly worn away, but what I recognized made me realize where I was. I was lying on the original council's meeting room table.

Underneath my dominant hand I felt one of the Originals names carved into the table. I ran my hand over the symbols and recognized it as Alakouse's. I sat up and slid over to the edge of the table. I looked down at my left arm and saw the vein of energy flowing through briefly until it faded and I remembered the erasing technique. I heard footsteps. Looking up, I stared into the Within's cold gray eyes. I slid to the floor and lost my balance, so I leaned against the table for support.

"I see stand and watch an abandoned servant to original remaining to fight." I said.

"You speak as original."

"Yes."

"You intend to keep as such?" he asked.

"It was my original days as a servant."

"So you were, servant turned councilor. I believe the first to achieve such rank."

"True and false. The others failed, I am the one to succeed. Besides you killed the rest through Alakouse's second in rank of servant."

"You even regain your original memories."

"Yes."

"I truly hate the Original's ways of speaking."

"I see."

He stared coldly at me, and then he appeared in front of me and held a dagger to my throat. I looked down at the dagger and saw some of his energy coursing through its blade.

"So the rule in the deal about not killing a councilor doesn't apply to you then?" I asked.

"Those rules say if one of you are a threat I may do as I please."

"Then why bring me back?"

"I...the Originals will pay for this."

"Perhaps...perhaps. Perhaps you will, but your servant will turn sides before you have that chance." I said.

"My servant is just that, a servant that will die by the end of this day."

"Maybe, although I believe if he dies it will be on his own terms."

"You have no power over my servant. You are just a pathetic servant from a dead era."

"You're right, the Originals era is dead, but I'm not just some pathetic servant. I'm Oyak the Councilor, the Councilors servant, the citizen, the One Who Should Not Be, and most of all, I am the one who will eventually kill you and take everything you have consumed."

"So that your true intentions."

"Only one small part of a more complex plan."

"You may be the One Who Should Not Be, but you are pathetic compared to me and that's all you ever will be, a pathetic creation that should be erased from existence."

"I will kill you. Not today, not anytime soon, but when I'm ready, I will kill you."

"You will never kill me, but you will make a worthy challenge in the future. Now I believe that my servant is about to be collected along with the last original. Farewell One Who Should Not Be. You may make a worthy challenge in the future."

He lifted the blade from my throat, opened a portal, and disappeared through it. I closed my eyes and found where Alakouse and Alexed were in the city. They were fighting at the end of the main crossroad that led from the tower. I opened a portal above Alexed and jumped through.

I opened my eyes and felt myself begin to fall. I unleashed an energy wave to slow my fall and to distract Alexed. I landed in front of Alexed and blocked a stab meant for Alakouse's heart. I grabbed Alexed's energy blade, absorbing all of its energy and sending him flying with that energy. I created an energy barrier around me and Alakouse. I summoned Vollenth, Zeon, and Jurrisk's hosts to my neck, and then turned to Alakouse.

"Hello Alakouse. It's been awhile since our last meeting."

"Oyak...the being refused to revive you, how are you here?"

"The thirteen within revived through the Within."

"Thirteen?"

"Yes...I believe we should speak of that later. Where is the rest of the council?"

"Oyak, don't change the subject."

"Ala...fine then. When you made the deal with the being, a small part of you was consumed, along with the memories of the true fates of the rest of the Originals."

"What happened to them?"

"Alakouse, this isn't the time."

"Then make time. I need to know this."

"Once the deal was made, all the Originals were killed excluding you, but the small piece I mentioned earlier was consumed to make up for it."

"I remember the selections, the original thirteen selections. I remember them. They aren't false."

"The Within can make his false seem real. He took away the memories of your top servants as well."

"How do I know that you aren't a pawn of the being?"

"Because"—I held out my left arm and showed him my left palm which still glowed dimly—"I doubt the being would've given me this technique."

"That's the...I see. Who gave you that?"

"The other within...along with the knowledge of zero."

"Zero...we'll discuss that piece later."

"Yes, I suppose we will...the rest of the council, where are they?"

"They're...scattered, mostly in the tunnels helping the citizens down to the deeper tunnels, although Velzeak is fighting Alexed's servants."

"Join the group and escort the rest of the citizens. I'll take care of Alexed."

"Oyak, this is my fight."

"Not anymore."

I transformed into my golden dragon form and connected with the rest of the true forms.

"Oyak, I won't run from Alexed."

"It's not your fight anymore Alakouse. Besides, if I let you finish your fight then Alexed would die."

"You're not planning on killing him?"

"No, not unless the Within fully takes him over."

"The being has already taken over, Oyak, he's—"

"He's your second servant in rank, I was your first. Both of us trained under all thirteen and that strength will be needed to fight the Within."

"I...Oyak, if you or Alexed were a servant, I would remember."

"I told you earlier that the memories of your top servants were taken away when you made the deal. I was the first servant to be trained under all thirteen Originals. Alexed was sixteenth given that honor. His skill was equal and sometimes better than mine so you gave him second rank."

"You really think he's worth saving after all he's responsible for killing?"

"Yes. If I get to him, he'll find ways to pay for what he's done in time."

"So I'll just forget about everything he's done?"

"No, you will not forget or forgive, but you will not slaughter my friend."

"You call one who slaughters citizen's friend?"

"No, I call the old Alexed my friend. If I can't fully revive him then I will kill him."

"He is just a pawn of the being. He will never be who you say he was again."

"Perhaps not, although it won't kill me to try."

"You're a fool Oyak. If you must waste the opportunity that the Originals gave you, then at least make sure you kill him while you senselessly try to talk him out of the act."

Alakouse opened a portal and walked through it. The portal closed and the barrier shattered. I was left alone with Alexed. I turned and stared at Alexed, my friend but also my enemy.

"Alexed, I believe we need to talk."

"I have no interest in talking."

"Yes, Within I'm quite aware of your presence. I wish to speak to Alexed, not you."

"What nonsense are you saying?"

"I can see your flow through veins."

"I'm impressed. I doubt even Alakouse could see through this."

"I suppose One Who Should Not Be has some advantages."

"You act as if that title is not a curse. I assure you it is."

"Perhaps."

"You truly are an annoyance, just like the rest of citizens and Councilors."

"Why make the deal then? Why not break it and destroy everyone with your own power instead of hiding behind your servants?"

"Because watching all of you pathetic beings suffer is more enjoyable than just killing all of you at once."

"Release Alexed. He's not yours to toy with."

"He made a deal with me for power. He is mine to toy with how I wish."

"No, he's a councilor's servant. As the only living councilor's servant with full access to my memories, he's my responsibility not yours."

"He traded away that right once he died."

"He regained it after he was revived."

"No, he belongs to me now not you."

"Release him being, or are you afraid that I'll be able to turn him to my side?"

"You will fail in every attempt, and at any rate, regardless of your actions, I will consume him at the end of this day."

"Release him and we'll see, Within."

"Very well then, let's see whose will is stronger."

Alexed's eyes returned to normal, and I felt the being's energy dissipate from his veins.

"Alexed, I know that your mind is fragmented and broken from the Within, but you must listen to me now."

Alexed just stared blankly at me and then charged at me. I dodged his attack and threw him to the ground, placing a barrier around him.

"Alexed, listen to me. I can save you from your death if you would just listen!" I yelled.

"Lies, lies, lies!" he yelled.

"I'm not lying! I can save you from death and heal your mind to its full capacity."

"My mind is whole."

"No...Alexed, do you remember the Zelkeref Council?" I asked.

"The...the Zelkeref Council were a group of citizens that formed a new type of council that disapproved of many of the Originals ideals. They also broke several regulations to make their point apparent."

"Yes. Do you remember who their leader was?" I asked.

"The leader was never captured, nor seen."

"You were the leader Alexed. You started it shortly after the first regulations were made."

"Lies."

"After I became a councilor's servant and was granted the ability to train under each councilor. You approached me. You asked me to join you and your council, and I accepted."

"More lies. Let me out of here so we can continue to fight until this city is rubble."

"Alexed, once I was a member, I was able to recommend you and several other members as candidates for becoming councilor's servants."

Alexed unleashed an energy wave that cracked the barrier but slammed him against the opposite side.

"Alexed, you must of noticed the dark patches in your mind. They are left over from when the being rearranged your memories after you broke your mind."

"My mind is whole."

"In the original era, we served under Alakouse. I was the first given the right to train under all the Councilors. You were the sixteenth but eventually, after proving yourself to be my equal and sometimes superior, you were given second rank under Alakouse."

"Release me, Councilor, so I can rip you apart along with the city. I serve no one and I never have."

I jumped back a few feet and released the barrier. I looked at him as I had back in the Original's days. Back then I looked up to him and even respected him, but now he was only a shell of his former self. When I looked at him now, I only saw hate for what he once loved.

"Enough talking. Let's fight and destroy this pathetic city in the process." he said.

"We will fight. We will fight."

Alexed unleashed a weak energy wave that I absorbed easily, but it was just a distraction. In that brief moment of distraction, he was able to close the short distance between us and slide a blade into my heart. I pulled away and flew into the air while the forms began to heal my wound. Alexed joined me there after my wounds were healed.

"How about we make a deal?"

"What could you possibly offer me?"

"I can offer you the fight you want."

"At what price?"

"No real price, just a mutual understanding that only one of us will walk away from this fight, and both of us will utilize all of our energy from here on out."

"Deal, Councilor."

I transformed back into my normal form and allowed all of the forms' energy to flow fully into me. Once I had fully absorbed a large portion of the forms' energy, I disconnected from them and activated the seal in my left palm. I felt the air ripple around me, and I felt all the energy in the air dry up.

Alexed stared at me and then smiled. From underneath his cloak he pulled a dark gray true forms crystal. I looked at the host and sensed over four thousand broken true forms. Their shadows began appearing all around us. They rapidly shifted in and out of sight. A dark gray aura appeared around Alexed, and I recognized it as the Within's energy. His energy flowed around him but it wasn't the Within, only his energy. Vollenth's energy began to flow around me, along with the other Untamable's.

"So the Untamable's nature finally comes out." Alexed said.

"No, not the Untamable's nature. My nature."

"Oh really? Well I guess you're just a broken lump of energy with barely any intelligence to speak."

"Insulting my forms won't anger me. I only wish you would of come to your senses sooner so you could be saved from death."

"If I die, you will as well."

"Perhaps."

"Enough talking. Let's finish this."

"Yes, it will be finished."

The fight went on and on for hours upon hours. Each move, every technique, shook the city and caused destruction throughout. Millions of citizen's homes were destroyed in the first few seconds of the fight, millions more followed as we continued. We held nothing back as we battled. I fully utilized every ounce of each of the forms' energy. Alexed used all of his broken forms energy to match almost all of my attacks. The attacks he didn't match, he brushed off with little change. We battled until neither of us could move.

"When you officially became a councilor's servant, we battled like this, although we didn't destroy the city as we both have now. We fought until both of us collapsed and slept for a week."

"Yes...yes we did."

"Alexed?"

"Only for a small time...I was able to reconnect myself."

"What...what are the Within's plans?"

"You...you know them. Kill me to stop them or, or you'll face the full force of the Within."

"I will take my chances with the Within. I need to send an old friend beyond with piece of mind."

"You...you always were a fool Oyak...your fight just got a hundred times harder."

"I...always like a challenge."

"I'll be devoured before the end. After I lose this, I'll be gone. Kill this worthless host when it's passed."

"Are there other servants?"

"He's...training one...farewell Oyak, my friend."

"Farewell Alexed, the Councilor's Servant."

I felt Alexed's lifeforce fade away and be replaced by a small piece of the Within's own lifeforce.

"You and everything else will die now." the being said through Alexed.

"That's where you are mistaken. The only being that has died is my friend Alexed, the Councilor's Servant."

"Alexed balkel shek—"

"Oyak melkel alk Alakouse Alexed felk elnor ek keather!" I yelled before the being could finish.

The technique took hold of both of us and held us in place while energy began flowing through the air and the forms connections regained their strength. I connected with the rest of the forms, creating a condensed energy orb between me and the being. I flowed all the energy I had within me into the orb and launched it at the being. The orb sent the being flying into the tower at the end of the crossroad. I gathered energy from the forms as I walked to the tower's courtyard. Once I arrived, the being had just gotten to his feet.

"Did you have a fun trip, Within?"

"I thought you would be a challenge, but you're just an annoyance. Die with the rest of everything."

"We'll see."

"Alexed balkel shek Alexed Alakouse balker sek!" he yelled.

"Melsek kelzer Zelk." I said.

The technique activated and I was able to connect to one of the few forms that was artificially created by the Originals. The form granted the user near instant speed at little energy cost. I took one step back, and I was near the end of the crossroad.

"Thank you." I said to the form.

"Velkereath." he growled.

"Thank you, Velkereath. Your abilities should help me in the future."

"They can. Do not lock me away."

"I won't. Join my true in his host for now until I make you your own."

"Thank you...thank you Councilor."

"Your welcome. You can call me Oyak."

"Very well, Oyak. Thank you again."

I closed my eyes and located Alakouse within the tunnels.

"Alakouse, I need the concept to assure destruction of destruction of the city."

"I will help. When you collide, I will join with you as concept and councilor as I do with Alakouse." Palex said.

"Don't kill my form, Oyak." Alakouse said.

"I don't plan to."

"You must match his energy while traveling. I will let you overtake him once I join." Palex said.

"Very well. Thank you Palex. Alakouse, if I'm destroyed, kill the Within for me."

"That's your fight not mine, Oyak."

"Very well. Then if I'm destroyed, you'll have to tear me out of the Within yourself."

"Good luck, Oyak."

"Thank you, First. Thank you."

I opened my eyes and saw that Alexed's technique had started to fully take hold. The technique worked by transforming the user into pure energy and then fully unleashing all of that energy. It then started condensing everything around it into a single point until it began consuming everything around it. Everything that was consumed fueled its continued existence. The only way to stop it was to have it collide with someone using the same technique but with more energy. Once they collide, they combine and cancel each other out, giving back their physical form to the users.

I began absorbing the forms' energy, and once I was close enough to Alexed's current energy pool, I jumped into the air and began being pulled towards Alexed's technique.

I kept picking up speed until all I saw around me was a blur. Vollenth helped me regain my sight, and all around me I saw pieces of citizen's homes flying towards his technique.

"Now Oyak!" all of the forms yelled.

"Oyak balkel shek Oyak Alakouse balker sek." I said as I collided with his technique.

I felt Palex flow most of his energy into me and for an instant, I felt invincible. Then the technique consumed all of it. Once I said the last word, the technique instantly stopped my movement and held me in place. I felt nothing at first, and then I felt everything fade away. Vollenth, the rest of the forms, and then my mind slowed. I could feel the technique unleash all of the energy I had gathered and then begin to condense it. I sensed Alexed close by, but I couldn't concentrate enough to find him. I felt our techniques fight for control and then fuse into one. Alexed appeared in front of me and then everything faded into white.

About the Author

Oyak Muisso Meakezy is the writer of the Creation Council Era, and it is his first commercial publishing. Oyak has been writing since elementary school and over the years has created multiple fantasy worlds within his head, but the Solstice Criterium world is his most expansive and most developed. Oyak lives in Virginia and is almost 19 years old at the time of publishing.

Contacts and links

Send any questions to solsticecriterium13@gmail.com

Check out more of my writing at http://www.writerscafe.org/prymore/

Check out my writing YouTube channel, solstice criterium libraries for more of my writing.

www.ingramcontent.com/pod-product-compliance
Lightning Source LLC
Chambersburg PA
CBHW070614130626
46556CB00001B/369